He shook his head, rewarding her with a slow smile.

"You're a little smart-ass."

"Ah, but I grow on you."

"We'll see."

"Are you looking for a job?"

"I have two jobs," he reminded her. "I'm a farrier and a physician's assistant. My services are in high demand on the rodeo circuit."

"They'd be pretty handy around the Double D, too."

"How long would you need me?"

"About three weeks." She sat up and took new interest. "You wouldn't have to stay around the whole time. Seriously. You could be on call."

"I'm not short on things to do."

"Neither am I. It's time that's the kicker, isn't it?"

"A day is a day. You fill it with how you feel."

"I couldn't've said it better. Right now, tonight…" She stretched her arms straight and strong, crooning a saucy "I fee-e-e-l good." She slid him a glance. "Hey, you're smiling."

"You're growin' on me."

Dear Reader,

A warm welcome back to the Double D Wild Horse Sanctuary!

When I started writing *One Cowboy, One Christmas* I had no idea that Sally Drexler was going to be such a strong character that she would demand her own book. But what a strong woman she turned out to be. Nothing will stop Sally from living her life to the fullest. She has a wonderful sense of humor, is completely committed to the wild horses that have taken over the Double D Ranch and she loves fiercely. She has learned to live in the moment because she can't be sure how she'll feel tomorrow. She's thrilled that her sister has found a love to last a lifetime, but she has no thought of discovering that kind of joy for herself.

Enter Hank Night Horse. Hank is a private man, one who has suffered losses of his own. He's a horseman, a healer, a man who gives without expecting—without even *wanting* much in return. Hank is my kind of hero. He's strong, complex, protective (particularly of his own heart) and oh, so cool.

If you're a horse lover like me, check out the Black Hills Wild Horse Sanctuary online. Douglas O. Hyde founded the program in 1988, and it is the inspiration for the Double D Wild Horse Sanctuary.

Now come with me to a place where wildness reigns and love conquers all.

All my best, always,

Kathleen

KATHLEEN EAGLE

COOL HAND HANK

Silhouette®

SPECIAL EDITION®

Published by Silhouette Books

America's Publisher of Contemporary Romance

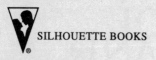

SILHOUETTE BOOKS

ISBN-13: 978-0-373-65506-9

COOL HAND HANK

Copyright © 2010 by Kathleen Eagle

Recycling programs
for this product may
not exist in your area.

Books by Kathleen Eagle

KATHLEEN EAGLE

published her first book, a Romance Writers of America Golden Heart Award winner, with Silhouette Books in 1984. Since then she has published more than forty books, including historical and contemporary, series and single-title, earning her nearly every award in the industry. Her books have consistently appeared on regional and national bestseller lists, including the *USA TODAY* list and the *New York Times* extended bestseller list.

Kathleen lives in Minnesota with her husband, who is Lakota Sioux. They have three grown children and three lively grandchildren.

For My Nieces and Nephews
and
To Honor the Memory of
Phyllis Eagle McKee

Chapter One

Hank Night Horse believed in minding his own business except when something better crossed his path. A naked woman was something better.

Technically, Hank was crossing her path. He was about to step out of the trees onto the lakeshore, and she was rising out of the lake onto the far end of the dock, but the breathtaking sight of her made her his business. She was as bold and beautiful as all outdoors, and she was making herself at home. Maybe she hadn't noticed the moonrise, couldn't tell how its white light made her skin gleam like a beacon on the water.

At his side, Phoebe saw her, too, but she knew better than to give their position away without a signal.

With all that skin showing, the woman looked edible. Phoebe was trying to decide whether to point or pounce. Hank knew his dog. He couldn't help smiling as the woman turned to reach for a towel hanging over a piling. She was slender but womanly, with a long, sleek back and a sweet little ass. If he moved, if he made the slightest sound, he would kill a perfect moment. It would be a shame to see her…

…stumble, flail, go down on one knee. From graceful to gawky in the blink of an eye, the woman plunged headlong into the lake without a sound issuing from her throat. Hank was stunned.

Phoebe took off like a shot, and their cover was blown.

Fall back, regroup, find new cover.

She had the water, and he had the dog. *Excuse my dog. She has no manners.* And the woman…

…should have surfaced by now. *Maybe the water had her.*

Phoebe was paddling to beat hell. Hank skittered sideways down the pine-needle-strewn path until his boots hit the dock, reminding him that whatever he was about to do, the boots had to go.

And then what? He was a man of many talents, but swimming wasn't one of them. If the adoption people had told him Phoebe lived for the water, he would have walked right past her and taken the Chihuahua in the next cage. Instead, he'd saddled himself with a big yellow bitch who thought she was a seal. Or a dolphin. Dolphins could rescue swimmers, couldn't they?

Dive, baby, dive.

Swish! The woman's head broke the water's surface like a popped cork. Phoebe paddled in a circle around her, yapping exuberantly as though she'd scared up some game.

The woman spat a water-filled "Damn!" toward the open lake as Phoebe circled in front of her. "Hey! Where'd you come from?"

"She's with me." The water sprite whirled in Hank's direction. "You okay?"

"Fine. Where did *you* come from?"

Hank jerked his chin toward his shoulder and the pine woods behind his back. "My dog—*Phoebe, get over here*—my dog thought I shot you."

The woman laughed. A quick, unexpected burst of pure glee, which Phoebe echoed, adding gruff bass to bright brass.

"Are you coming in, too?"

He hadn't thought it through. Hadn't even realized he was sitting at the end of the dock with one boot half off. "Not if I don't have to. It looked like you fell."

"I did." Eyeing him merrily, she pushed herself closer with one smooth breast stroke. Her pale body glimmered beneath the rippling water. "I have fins for

arms and two left feet that want to be part of a tail."
She looked over at the dog paddling alongside her.
"I'm not dead in the water. Sorry, Phoebe."

"She thought you were flapping your wings. If you
really had fins, she wouldn't've bothered."

"But you would have?"

He pulled his boot back on. "The way you went
down, I thought you'd had a heart attack or something."

"Klutz attack." She bobbed in place now, her arms
stirring the water just beneath the surface. She made
not going under look deceptively easy. "The water's
fine once you get used to it. Now that I'm back in I
wouldn't mind company."

"You've got some." He glanced straight down.
Booted feet dangled over dark water. *Damn*. He felt
like he was the one caught with his pants down. Had
to get up now. He'd recover his dignity once he had
something solid underfoot. Needed something to hang
on to, and words were all he had. *Keep talking*. "That
dog won't hunt, but she sure loves to swim."

"And you?"

He scooted toward the piling. "I'm not givin' up the
best seat in the house." *Until I can grab that post.*

"So you're one of those guys who'd rather look
than leap."

"I'm one of those guys who'd rather watch than
drown."

There was that laugh again, warm and husky, like

an instrument played well and often. "And you were going to save me exactly how?"

"By throwin' you a life boot." He smiled, more for his hand striking the post than his wit striking her funny.

"No need to." Her voice echoed in the night. "My feet are touching bottom."

"You serious?"

"If I stood up, the water would only be up to my waist."

"From what I saw, that would make it about two feet deep."

"Come try it out." She dared him with a wicked, deep-throated chuckle. "Bring your depth finder."

What a sight. The strange woman and the dog he fed every damn day were treading in tandem, two against one. Phoebe should have known better.

"I've got a measuring stick." Hank grinned. "But it retracts in the cold."

"Speaking of cold…" She hooked her arm over Phoebe's shoulders. "If you're not going to join us, I'd like to take another stab at getting out."

Post in hand, he stood. "My feet are touching bottom."

"Not mine."

"Yours is wet." He laid his hand on the towel she'd left hanging over the post. "Bring it up here and I'll dry it for you."

"One free look is all you get, cowboy. A second will cost you."

"How much?"

With the pounding of her fist she sent a waterspout into his face. He staggered back as Phoebe bounded onto the lakeshore.

"Damn! You must have ice water in your veins, woman."

"Warm hands, cold heart. Go back where you came from, please." She assumed a witchy pitch. "And your little dog, too."

If he could've, he would've. Back to the little house in the North Dakota hills where he'd grown up, where his brother lived with his wife and kids, and where the only water anybody had to worry about was spring runoff. Even though he liked the Black Hills—what red-blooded Lakota didn't?—he wasn't big on weddings or wild women. But Hank Night Horse was a man who kept his word.

He touched the brim of his hat. "Nice meeting you."

So this was what a *real* wedding was all about.

Hank scanned the schedule he'd been handed at the Hilltop Lodge reception desk along with the key to a room with "a great view of the lake." He'd told Scott—the host, according to the badge on the blue jacket—he'd already had a great view at the lake. Scott had promised him an even better one at sunrise, and Hank said he wouldn't miss it. But a wedding was something else. He'd witnessed a few horseback weddings sandwiched between rodeo events, and he'd stood up for one of his cousins in front of a judge, but he'd never actually watched a guy jump through so many hoops just to trade promises.

Damn. A three-day schedule? His friend had claimed to be done with weekend-event schedules now that he'd hung up his spurs, but you'd never know it by the list Hank was looking at now. Social hour, wedding rehearsal, rehearsal dinner. He had to laugh at the thought of a rodeo cowboy publicly practicing his walk down the aisle. The sound of Western-boot heels crossing the wood floor brought the picture to life.

"What's so funny, Horse?" Zach Beaudry clapped a hand on Hank's shoulder. "You laughin' at me? You wait till it's your turn."

"For this?" Grinning, Hank turned, brandishing the flower-flocked paper beneath his friend's nose. "If you don't draw a number, you don't take a turn."

"My advice?" Zach snatched the schedule and traded it for a handshake. "Take a number. You don't wanna miss the ride of a lifetime."

"Here's two, just for you. Number one, I patch you cowboys up for a living. I know all about that *ride of a lifetime.* And number two…" Hank gave his starry-eyed friend a loose-fisted tap in the chest. No man wore his heart on his sleeve quite like a lovesick cowboy. "Nobody's askin' you for advice this weekend, Beaudry.

It's like asking the guy holding the trophy how he feels about winning."

"Damn, you're a smart-ass. Be careful you don't outsmart yourself. Come meet my family."

Hank followed Zach through a lobby full of rustic pine furniture, leather upholstery, and glass-eyed trophy heads. Rough-hewn beams supported the towering ceiling, and a fieldstone fireplace dominated one wall. They passed through a timber-framed archway into a huge dining room—bar at one end, dance floor at the other, rectangular tables scattered in between—flanked by enormous windows overlooking the lake. Hank wondered whether the shoreline was visible from the terrace beyond the massive glass doors. According to the plaque in the front entry, the lodge and the lakefront were products of a Depression-era Federal construction project, and everything about them was rough-hewn, but grand.

"This is my bride," Zach was saying, and Hank turned from the windows to the woman linking arms with her man. "Annie, Hank Night Horse."

She was small and pretty, and her smile seemed a little too familiar. But the way it danced in her blue eyes didn't connect, didn't feel like it had anything to do with him. And her curly golden ponytail looked bone dry. Hank held his breath and offered a handshake.

"Our wedding singer," the bride said in a soft, shy voice. "Thank you for coming, Hank."

"Sure." And relieved. He was sure he'd never heard the voice before, so he looked his buddy in the eye and smiled. "You did well, Beaudry."

"I did, didn't I?" Zach put his arm around his intended. "She's got a sister."

"You don't say." Hank lifted one shoulder. "I'm willing to sing for a piece of your wedding cake, but that's as far as I go."

"I'm just sayin', you got a great solo voice, man, but that solo livin' gets old."

"I'll bet it does. I know I don't like to go anywhere without Phoebe."

"She's here? Phoebe's here?" Zach's face lit up like a kid who smelled puppy. "Annie, if we can't get married on horseback, how 'bout we put Phoebe in the wedding party? She could carry the rings. She's like the physician's assistant's assistant. Hank's pretty good with his hands, but Phoebe's got heart. He's stitchin' a guy up, she's lovin' him up like only man's best friend knows how to do. Helps you cowboy up so you can climb back on another bull."

"He can't," Ann assured Hank. "We wrote it into the contract."

"That's good, 'cause I'm tired of sewing him up and watching him rip out my stitches in the next go-round."

"Where's Phoebe?" Zach demanded. "I'll bet she's not tired of me."

"She's outside. Caused me some trouble, so she's in the doghouse."

"No way. You tell Phoebe she can—" Zach glanced past Hank and gave a high sign. "Sally! Over here! I want you to meet somebody."

"Can he swim?"

That was the voice. "Sounds like I'm out of my depth again." Hank turned and hit her feet first with a gaze that traveled slowly upward, from the red toenails she'd claimed to be touching bottom to the blue neckline that dipped between pale breasts. He paused, smiled, connected with her eyes—blue, but more vibrant than her sister's—and paid homage again with the touch of his finger to the brim of his hat. Her short blond hair looked freshly fixed. "I like your dress."

"What's that? You like me dressed?"

"That, too. But clothes don't make the woman." He'd already seen what did.

"So true. I didn't catch your name."

"Hank Night Horse."

Ann looked up at Zach. "I have a feeling we missed something."

"I have a feeling this is the sister," Hank said as he offered his hand. Hers was slight and much colder than advertised. He gave it a few extra seconds to take on a little heat. He had plenty to spare.

"And this is the music man." Sounding as cool as her hand felt, Sally looked him straight in the eye. For someone who'd been laughing it up less than an hour ago, she sure wasn't giving him much quarter.

"Hank, Sally Drexler, soon to be my sister-in-law. Have you two already…"

"I took Phoebe for a walk right after we pulled in. She tried to retrieve Sally from the lake."

"Aw, you gotta love Phoebe," Zach said cheerfully. "Hank's part of the medical team working the rodeo circuit, and Phoebe's his bedside manner."

Sally's eyes brightened. "I've spent a lot of time around the rodeo circuit. I used to be a stock contractor. Zach delivered the thrills and I furnished the spills. But that was probably before your time."

"I just hand out the pills."

"He does a lot more than that," Zach said. "Pops joints back in place, sets bones, makes the prettiest stitches you ever saw. Plus, he shoes horses on the side."

Sally challenged Hank's credentials with a high-headed smile. "All that and a wedding singer, too?"

"First time." Hank gave Ann an indulgent smile. "I hear brides can be hard to please, and I'm a what-you-hear-is-what-you-get kind of a guy. I don't mind being the funeral singer. You get no complaints from the star of the show."

"You're listed on the program without the name of the song, which I really wanted…" Ann glanced at Zach. They were already developing their own code.

Good start, Hank thought. He and his former wife had never gotten that far.

"But we agreed to leave it up to you," Zach filled in.

"It's my gift. I want it to be a surprise."

Ann shrugged. "I promise not to complain."

"I promise not to sing 'Streets of Laredo.'" Hank glanced across the room. A handful of people were gathered at the bar. Two women were setting bowls of flowers on the white-draped table. He turned to Sally. "What's your wedding assignment?"

"Maid of honor, of course. It's a plum role. By the way," she reported to her sister, "more gifts were delivered here today. I had the desk clerk store them under lock and key. There's actually one from Dan Tutan."

Tutan. Hank frowned. He hadn't heard the name since he was a kid, when he'd heard it whispered respectfully, sometimes uneasily, eventually contemptuously around the Night Horse home.

"Or his wife," Ann was saying. "She takes neighborliness seriously."

"Dan Tutan's your neighbor?" Hank asked.

Sally sighed. "A few miles down the road. Not close enough so we have to see him every day. But before I say *fortunately,* is he a friend of yours?"

"Nope."

"Well, he'd like to turn our wild-horse sanctuary into a dog-food factory."

"Why's that?"

"The horses like to mess with him," Zach said. "They know he's extremely messable."

"Tutan's had a pretty sweet deal on grazing leases around here for so long he's forgotten what a lease is," Sally said. "We're bidding on some leases and some grazing permits that he's held for years, and we've got a good chance at them because of the sanctuary. We're a retirement home for unadoptable wild horses. We give them grassland instead of a Bureau of Land Management feedlot. So Tutan doesn't like us much these days. How do you know him?"

"My father knew him." Hank glanced away. "Tutan wouldn't know me from an Indian-head penny."

"He'd know the penny," Sally said. "Damn Tootin' never walks away from any kind of money."

Zach clapped a hand on Hank's shoulder. "Don't tell him which one we picked up for a song."

"*Damn Tootin'.*" Hank chuckled. He didn't think he'd heard that one.

"Were they friends?" Sally asked. "Your father and my neighbor?"

"My dad worked for Tutan for a while. Long time ago. No, they weren't friends."

"Good. I'm not good at watching what I say about people I hate." Sally linked arms with her sister. "I'd get the bomb squad to check out his gift if I were you. And then put it in the regifting pile."

"Tell us how you really feel, Sally," Zach teased. He winked at Hank. "I'm glad you're giving us live music. That's something she can't regift."

"I'm recording everything," Sally said. "Hell, if your singer's any good, I'll burn a few CDs for Christmas presents. The frugal rancher's three R's: regift, repurpose, recycle." She poked Zach in the chest as though she were testing for doneness. "But we can't regift your brother's trip, so you're going to use that one."

"We'll get to it. There's no rush."

"No rush to go on your honeymoon?" Sally flashed Hank a smile. "What's this guy's problem, Doc?"

"Can't say."

"You're ducking behind that confidentiality screen, aren't you?" She turned back to Zach. "Your extremely wealthy brother hands you the extreme honeymoon, the wedding trip of your dreams, the one you mapped out with your bride, and you're saying *we'll get to it?* Like *anytime* is honeymoon time?"

"Well, isn't it?" Zach held up a cautionary hand. "Hold on, now, I haven't said *I do* yet. I gotta go work on those vows some more, make sure we both say *I do it anytime. All the time. Rain or shine.*"

The bride blushed.

The maid of honor laughed. "Say what you want, cowboy. I figure a nice long, romantic honeymoon will guarantee me a niece or nephew nine months later. If you don't get away from the Double D, what you'll do is exactly what you've been doing, which is working your fool britches off."

"*Britches off* is step one, Sally," Zach said. "It's not much work, and it's no guarantee, but it's a start. Right, Hank?"

Hank answered his friend with a look. The conversation had veered into no-comment land.

"I can handle the Double D." Sally glanced back and forth between Zach and Ann. "I'm *fine*."

"We're here for a wedding," Ann said, "which is a one-time thing, and we're doing it up right. Right here. Right now. We're going to rehearse." Ann offered a hand for the taking. "Hank?"

"You want me to practice walkin' and talkin', fine." Hank took the bride's hand with a smile. "But I don't rehearse my songs in public. It's bad luck."

"Let's walk and talk, then. Help me make a list of reasons why Zach should ride horses instead of bulls."

Sally hung back, watching her sister walk away with two attractive men. Two cowboys. Lucky Annie. As far as Sally was concerned, there were only two kinds of men out West: cowboys and culls. She didn't know any men from back East.

Sally had been around a lot of cowboys, and most of them were pretty easy to figure. All you had to do was take a look at the shirt. A cowboy wore his heart on his sleeve and a number on his back. He lived day to day and traveled rodeo to rodeo, accumulating cash and consequences. He was addicted to adrenaline, and he'd paid dearly for his sky-highs with rock-bottom lows. By the time he'd filled his PRCA permit with enough wins to earn the right to call himself a Professional Rodeo Cowboy, he'd paid in some combination of torn flesh, spilled blood and broken bone.

Such was the story of Zach Beaudry. He'd been the up-and-coming bull rider to beat until he'd met up with the unbecoming end of a bull's horn. Like the rest of his kind, he knew how to tough it out. Hunker down and cowboy up. Put the pieces back together and get back on the road. Which had led him to Annie's doorstep.

Hank Night Horse had the look of a cowboy. He was lean and rangy, built to fork a horse and cut to the chase. But a full place setting required a spoon. Sally smiled to herself as she pictured his possibilities. He looked great going away. She could paste herself against that long, tapered back and snug her thighs under his, tuck his tight butt into her warm bowl and be fortified. She could back up to him and invite him to curl his strong body around her brittle one and make her over. It could happen. In her dreams, anyway.

Hank turned to say something to Annie, who turned to say something to Zach and then back to Hank again. Conspiring. Setting Sally up. She knew what they were up to, and she didn't mind as long as this crazy body of hers was working properly. The fall from the dock hadn't been a good sign, but she was back in control now. And Hank Night Horse was turning back, giving her another one of those rousing once-overs. *You and me, woman.* He was coming for her, and, ah! she saw how fine he looked coming and knew how readily and happily she would come and come and come if the table were set with a man like Hank Night Horse. It wouldn't matter how much time he had to spare as long as it was—what was the expression? *Quality time.* Remission from illness was like a blue space between clouds. Either make the most of it, or stay in your box.

"Care to join me in the back row?" he asked.

"Am I your assignment?" She threw her voice into her sister's key. "If you're not going to rehearse your song, could you keep an eye on Sally?"

"I didn't quite catch what they said," he claimed with a twinkle in his eye. "Something about *drink.* I'm supposed to buy you one or keep you from falling in. Either way, I could be in for some trouble. Are you a troublemaker, Sally?"

"I do my best. And I know you're lying, because I'm not allowed to drink."

"Anything?"

"Anything with alcohol in it."

"Who said anything about alcohol?" He gave her a challenging look, his eyes growing darker and hooded, his full lips twitching slightly, unwilling to smile. "And who makes the rules?"

"Sensible Sally." She gave the smile he denied her. "That was her alter ego down at the lake. Shameless Sally."

"She's got the right idea. Shame shouldn't be allowed, either." He tucked his thumbs into the front pockets of his jeans. "So, what'll it be?"

She looked at her watch. "Rehearsal in five. Can't hardly whip up a good batch of trouble in five minutes. Sensible Sally drinks green tea on the rocks with a twist."

Hank decided to "make that two," and they left the dining room, glasses in hand, no hurry in their feet. Sally felt a growing reluctance to catch up with the little wedding party in the lodge library. The lakeside setting for the ceremony would be set up tomorrow, so tonight's indoor rehearsal was literally a dry run. Sally knew her part. She'd seen it played out a hundred ways in movies, read the scene in dozens of books. Sensible Sally stayed in the house a lot. Shameless Sally couldn't go out to play until the unreliable body caught up with the willing spirit, and now that the two were working in tandem, she would go where the spirit moved her.

"Look!" She pointed to a window, grabbed Hank's arm and towed him out the front door on to the huge covered porch. A procession of trail riders passed under the yard lights on their way to the pasture below the lodge. "How was the ride?" Sally called out.

"Beautiful!" said one of the helmeted riders. "Made it to the top of Harney Peak."

"Let's go up there tomorrow," Sally said to Hank. "You ride, don't you? We should…" She turned to the riders. "Where did you get the horses?"

"We brought our own. We're a club."

"But there's a hack stable close by," said the last rider as she passed under the light. "Ask at the desk."

Sally looked up at Hank. "We could go really early." She turned, cupped her hand around her cheek and shouted at the last rider's back. "How long did it take?"

"All day!"

Sally scowled. "I'll bet I could take a marker to the programs and change the time. The lake is beautiful this time of day. *Night*." She pointed to the white moon hovering above the ponderosa pines. "It'll be full tomorrow. Imagine Annie in her white gown, and Zach…well, he's wearing black, but can't you just see it? Moonlight on the lake?"

"I did, yeah. Beautiful."

"They don't need us. They wouldn't even notice. Look." She took his hand and led him to the end of the porch, pointed to the tall, bright corner windows that showcased the rehearsal getting under way in the library.

Sally could see Zach's niece and nephew perusing the bookshelves that flanked the stone fireplace. Zach was having a chat with his brother, Sam. Annie and the minister were poking through a sheaf of papers. "My baby sister's getting married tomorrow," she whispered. Hard to believe. The window might have been a movie screen, except that she knew these people—some better than others—and what they were doing was exactly what they'd been talking about for months. It was happening. Sally's little sister was getting married. "They won't notice anyone but each other tomorrow." She squeezed Hank's hand. "Let's do it."

"Do it?"

"Tomorrow. Let's ride to the top of Harney Peak."

"Zach's a good man. They don't come much better."

"Oh, I know that." She drew a deep breath and laughed. "But I love the smell of horse in the morning."

He laughed with her, and that felt good. Even better when he took control of the hand-holding and led her back into the lodge as though they were in this together, a two-part unit joining a group of two-and-more-part units. She could come to like this man much more than Sensible Sally would normally permit.

The first person they ran into when they entered the library was the wizened cowboy who would be giving

Annie away. Hoolie was draped over a pair of crutches near the door, prompting Sally to ask gently whether his ankle was bothering him again, whether he was coming or going.

"Thinkin' about getting outta the way until they decide what they want me to do. One of them kids tripped and near busted my cast."

"It was an accident," the sandy-haired boy called out over the top of the book he'd been reading.

"Man, they can hear good when they want to, can't they?" the wiry cowboy muttered, glancing at Hank. Then he turned to the boy. "I know you're sorry, Jim. No hard feelings. I can still hobble."

"Hank, this is Henry Hoolihan, our foreman."

"Hoolie." He offered Hank his hand. "Nobody's called me Henry since I was Jim's age. Who dug that up?"

"I don't know, but it's on the program," Sally said. "Jim and Star are Zach's brother's kids. Say hello to Hank Night Horse, Zach's doctor."

The children sang out as instructed, but Hoolie said, "Doctor?"

Hank glanced at Hoolie's cast. "I work the rodeo circuit as a physician's assistant. Zach's been a pretty steady customer the last few seasons." As one, the three turned their attention to the couple attending to wedding business on the far side of the room. "He's a good hand."

"Was," Sally said. "He says he's retiring."

"The body can only take so much," Hank said. "Some guys don't know when to quit. I'm glad Zach's not one of those guys." He looked at Sally. "He's still a good hand."

"We love Zach," Sally said with a smile. "Don't we, Hoolie? I'm being summoned. Let's get this over with so we can eat. And then on to the fun stuff." She touched Hank's sleeve. "Keep your program handy. We had one dull moment scheduled in, but then you came along and buffed it up, thank you very much."

"The pleasure was mine." He eyed her hand and then raised his dark gaze to her eyes as he leaned close to her ear. "Seein' as how the buff was yours."

Sally's neck tingled. An icy-hot shiver blew apart and streaked gloriously throughout her body. She stood still, waiting for the feel of another warm, magic breath.

"Sally, we need you!"

She let her hand slide to the edge of Hank's cuff where she could feel his working-man's skin. "Hold that thought," she said.

At dinner, Sally did her maid-of-honor duty by making the rounds among family and friends. Sally and Ann had lived on the Drexler ranch in South Dakota all their lives. But the family had been reduced to the two of them, along with Hoolie, who had come to work for their father before they were born, outlived him, and earned the privilege of giving the bride away.

And now they had Zach, who brought his mother, Hilda, and brother, Sam, to the Drexler fold—hardly big enough to fold—along with Sam's new wife, Maggie, and their two children. But the Beaudrys made their home in Montana, and Zach had become a rolling stone until he'd rolled to a stop at the Double D. The wedding was Zach's reunion with the Beaudrys as well as his formal initiation into the Drexler clan. The Beaudrys couldn't contain their joy, and why try?

Duty done in the middle of the circle, Sally moved to the edge, where Hank had laid claim to the observer's station, a post she had come to know all too well in recent years. She had made her peace with it, while Hank seemed quite comfortable there. Maybe he could teach her something. He'd moved from the table where they'd shared dinner with Hoolie and Hilda to a corner conversation area near the bar. When he saw her coming, he moved again, from a big leather chair to a love seat. She was invited.

"They're all going on a moonlight hayride," she reported as she sat down. "I'm supposed to fetch you."

He smiled. "Good luck."

"Ready for another dull moment?"

"Looking forward to it." He lifted his arm over her head and laid it along the back of the love seat. "You?"

"I don't feel like changing clothes. When I take these off, that'll be it for the night."

"Big day tomorrow."

"Big day." She laid her head back and let it rest against his arm. "They're good people, aren't they? Why would Zach stay away from home so long?"

"Wouldn't know."

"But you know him well enough to vouch for his character."

"Yep." He shifted a little closer. "Tell me more about your mustang sanctuary. How do you support it?"

"We get some support from federal programs. Before my dad died, the Double D was one of the biggest cattle ranches in the state, and we still have a small cow-calf operation. We're also permitted to sell some of the colts off the wild mares."

"Is there much of a market these days?"

"They sell pretty well if they're at least green broke. Even better if they're broke to ride. But the market fluctuates with the rest of the economy, and right now it's tough. I have a plan, but I put it on hold for the wedding."

"Is that why they're holding off on the honeymoon?"

"Oh, no." She turned her head to give him a warning glance. "They don't know I have a new plan in the works. They're trying to put the honeymoon on hold because they don't want to leave me—" she raised her brow and gave a suggestive little smile "—to my own devices."

"Sounds like you have a reputation."

"I did, but I haven't been keeping up. A reputation

is something you have to tend, just like a garden." She made growing, blooming, stepping-out gestures. "You want it to get big enough to precede you."

"Except when you get caught with your pants down."

"Depends on your perspective." She turned up the tease in her smile. "I can't speak for yours, but from mine, sooner or later you'll get my attention. It's better if you're not a *sooner.* Laters are generally slower and longer."

He shook his head, rewarding her with a slow smile. "You're a little smart-ass."

"Ah, but I grow on you."

"We'll see." But he crossed his near leg over the far one before she had a chance. "You can't hire somebody to help out while they're honeymooning?"

"Are you looking for a job?"

"I have two jobs," he reminded her. "I'm a farrier and a physician's assistant. My services are in high demand on the rodeo circuit."

"They'd be pretty handy around the Double D, too. If we had someone like you on staff, Zach and Annie would leave tomorrow. The day after at the latest."

"How big…how *many* on your staff?"

"Four, counting Hoolie. We get volunteers to work with some of the horses, but a lot of them are kids. Mostly from the reservation. Annie teaches at the high school."

"How long did they plan to be gone?"

"About three weeks. But then Hoolie got tangled up in some barbed wire and broke his ankle." She sat up and took new interest. "You wouldn't have to stay around the whole time. Seriously. You could be on call."

"That's why I'm not on any kind of staff. Been there, done that, found out I don't much like being on call. You work a rodeo, you're there for the weekend. The pay's good, and you get to have a life."

"Doing what? You have a family?" She hadn't missed something, had she?

"I used to be married. Had a son. He died."

"Oh. I'm so sorry."

"Yeah, me, too. But I got my life back, and I'm not short on things to do."

"Neither am I. It's time that's the kicker, isn't it?"

"I probably don't think of time the same way you do."

No kidding. "Not very many people do."

"A day is a day. You fill it with how you feel."

"That's interesting. I couldn't've said it better. Right now, tonight…" She stretched her arms straight and strong, crooning a saucy, "I feeeel good." She slid him a glance. "Hey, you're smiling."

"You're growin' on me."

Chapter Two

"Oh, Annie."

Sally's sister turned from the mirror, eyes shining like stars. Her golden hair was swept up from the sides and anchored by a pearl-encrusted comb and a cascading veil. The off-the-shoulder neckline and body-skimming lines of her elegant ivory dress were simple and stunning and perfectly suited to the woman who stood there, eclipsing all the dreams the two sisters had conjured over the years.

The photographer quietly snapped pictures, allowing the moment to unfold. Sally was dumbfounded. How many times had they gotten dressed together, given each other a last-minute review? Sally had helped Annie choose each piece of her wedding ensemble, had overseen the fittings and giggled with her over their memories of dresses and dates, new measurements and old tastes, the never-ending Double D "chest jest"—a size Annie had at one time nearly reached—and the ever-after girlish dreams. And now all the pieces had come together, adding up to a vision that came as no real surprise to Sally even as it brought rare tears to her eyes. This was it. Annie was the fairy-tale bride.

Blinking furiously, Sally handed over the bouquet of white calla lilies, drew a deep breath and blew a wobbly whistle. "Whoa. Wow. Okay, Hoolie thinks he can get by without crutches, but I know what it's like to fall on your face in front of an audience, so I think we should put my cane in his hand right when the music starts."

"It's not a long walk. A few steps. I'm almost there, Sally." Annie grabbed Sally's hand, and the camera hummed. "Why am I shaking like this?"

"They're big steps." Baby sister was taking big steps, and Sally was the only Drexler left to hold her hand.

She wanted to hug her, hold her a little longer, but she made do with squeezing her hand rather than making smudges or wrinkles or tears. Annie wasn't leaving, but life would be different after today.

"I wonder if *he's* nervous. Do you think he's shaking like this?" Annie laughed and shook her head. "Probably not. He's a cowboy. He rides...*used to* ride bulls for a living. What's a little—" she turned for another glance in the mirror, complete with bouquet, and smiled "—wedding?"

"There's no such thing as a *little* wedding," Sally said, speaking from her all-too-frequent experience as a captive TV watcher. "By the numbers, this one is little. But it's big by my calculations."

"I know. It's all Sam's fault."

"I'm not calculating in dollars. Zach's brother's money definitely falls into the easy-come-easy-go category, and since there's so much of it, why not enjoy the frills? I'm talking about *big,* as in big as life. This is your wedding, and it means the world to me."

Sally touched the simple strand of pearls around her sister's neck. They had belonged to their mother, whom Sally saw so unmistakably in Annie's big, soft eyes and bow-shaped mouth and dainty chin. Sally looked more like their father, but she was the one who clearly remembered Mom. Sally was the keeper of Drexler memories.

"I'll be kinda glad when it's all…" Annie gave her head a quick toss. "No, I'm glad now. I'm ready. I feel beautiful. And you look beautiful, Sally." Annie turned her sister so that the mirror made a framed portrait unlike any they'd taken together before. They'd been big and lively, little and sweet. One primary, one pastel. One ready to go first, the other pleased to follow.

"I love you so much," Annie whispered, and Sally had no doubt. But Annie was the one once meant to wait while Sally went ahead. And it wasn't that Sally was resentful of the reversal—she really did look good in her chic, fluid blue waterfall of a dress, Annie's gift of opals around her neck and studding her ears, fragrant gardenias in her hair—but she was unsure of her footing. Annie was taking a big step.

Where did that leave Sally?

"Me, too, you," she said as she squeezed that ever-dependable hand again. "Lest we spoil the makeup, consider yourself kissed."

"You know you're not losing a sister, don't you? You're gaining a brother. And we're not going anywhere. We're partners, and we're family, and we're going to—"

"—be late for your wedding. Listen. I am fine." She enunciated each word forcefully, willing her sister to make sense of three simple words and move on. "Look at me. No cane, no pain." *Enjoy this with me while it lasts.* She needlessly fluffed Annie's veil. "This is your day, honey. Take a deep breath. Your man is out there waiting and, yes, probably feeling just the way you are. When you take each other's hands…" Sally smiled, blinking furiously because she *would not cry.* "Tell me what it's like, okay? That moment."

Annie nodded as she pulled her hand free, placed

a finger lightly at the outside corner of Sally's eye, caught a single tear and touched it to her lips.

Granite spires bound the crystalline-blue lake on the far side, the perfect backdrop for a hand-woven red willow arch decked out with a profusion of flowers. Guests were seated in white folding chairs. Zach's niece led the way, tossing handfuls of white rose petals on a path of fresh green pine needles. Sally followed, taking measured steps in time with the string quartet's elegant processional. Looking as handsome and relaxed in his black tux as he did in well-worn jeans, Zach waited for his bride. His brother, Sam—a little taller, a little darker, a little less at ease—stood like a sentry overseeing his charges. Daughter, son, wife, mother, brother—Sam's eyes attended to each one. He was clearly the Beaudry caretaker. *Funny,* Sally thought. *That's Annie, not me.*

Before she'd been diagnosed with multiple sclerosis, Sally had been the seeker, the doer, the risk taker. She'd cared passionately, but she'd never *taken care.* That was Annie's role. Careful, care-giving, selfless Annie.

Sally paused before the minister and looked the groom in the eye. *Be good to her, Zach. Be the man she deserves.* She pivoted and took her place, knowing she'd made her point. She felt Annie step up to fill the space she and Zach had left for her, but she couldn't quite turn to watch Hoolie place her sister's hand in Zach's. It was enough to see the movement from the corner of her eye, where Annie had touched her for a tear.

It was happening. Annie was interlacing her life with someone new, becoming someone else's next of kin. Sally clutched two handfuls of flowers and listened to identical promises exchanged in voices that complemented each other in a way she hadn't heard before. It was a pure sound and a simple truth. Annie and Zach belonged together.

And they stood together, hand in hand, while Hank played an acoustic guitar and sang "Cowboy, Take Her Away" in a deep, resonant voice that was made for a love song. He'd said his gift was his song, and he sang to the couple as though no one else was there and every note, every word had been written just for them. Sally was enchanted. Her beautiful sister, her new brother, the music and the man who made it—she wanted to suck it all in and keep it alive within her in a way that the video camera could never do.

At the end of the song, Hank said, "Kiss her, Zach." And he did, cheered on by friends and family, who showered them with white rose petals as they retreated down the path. The guests followed, and the violinists made merry music at the back of the line as it wended its way up a gentle slope between stands of tall pines. When they reached the lodge's gravel driveway, Zach swept his bride up in his arms and carried her across the path and up the steps to the front porch, where he set her down and kissed her again. Women sighed. Men whooped. Cowboy hats sailed skyward.

Annie and Zach were hitched.

"You're a lucky man." Sally raised her glass of sparkling water in toast.

"Yeah, I know." Sam put his arm around his new wife, Maggie. "I hit the jackpot."

Maggie looked up at him. "*You* did?"

"Trusted you and got myself a whole family."

"I think Sally's talking about winning the lottery," Maggie said. "It's crazy. Real people don't win the lottery."

"Well, it was complicated," Sam said. "It was Star's mother's ticket—our daughter, Star—but she died before she could claim it. In fact, we thought the damn thing was lost in a car accident, but it turned up, kinda like…" He waved his hand as though words failed.

"Miraculously," Maggie supplied.

"To put it mildly," Sam said. "It's been a year, but it still doesn't seem real. We're trying to manage it sensibly. You don't want to go crazy. You want to put some of it to good use now, give some away, make sure there's plenty left for the kids. I've never known any rich people, never thought I'd like them much."

"He won't give up his job," Maggie said.

Sam laughed. "She won't, either."

"I'm part-time now, but our little clinic needs nurses, and I'm a good one. We just moved into a house we built on Sam's land. It's a gorgeous spot." Maggie made a sweeping gesture. "Kind of like this, but the lake is smaller and the mountains are bigger. You have to come for a visit."

"Where's Hank?" Sam asked, searching over the heads of the guests. "Man, that guy can sing. He about killed my brother with that song." He grinned at Zach. "He didn't leave yet, did he?"

Did he?

Sally hugged her new brother-in-law. "Where's Hank?"

"I'll tell you a little secret about ol' Hank. He don't like compliments. He does his thing, and then he disappears for a while. He sang at a funeral once—bull rider, wrecked his pickup. Hank tore everybody up singin' over that kid. And then he disappeared. I found him playin' fetch with Phoebe." Zach glanced over the balcony railing. "He's around."

"Hey, cowboy." Annie joined the group, entwining her arm with her new husband's and beaming up at him as though he'd just hung the moon. "Take me away."

A skyward glance assured Sally that the moon wasn't up yet. The sun had slipped behind the trees, but there was still plenty of light for searching the grounds. She didn't have to go far. She found Phoebe first. The dog greeted her with a friendly bark, and the man followed, emerging from a stand of pines near a picnic table. He carried his jacket slung over his shoulder, white shirtsleeves rolled halfway up his forearms, black hat tipped low on his forehead.

Sally scratched Phoebe behind the ears and caught a little drool in the process. Hank tapped his thigh, and the dog heeled. With a hand signal, he had her sitting.

"Impressive," Sally said.

"She's willing to humor me because you're not as appealing as you were last night. If you were splashing around in the lake she'd be all over you."

"And you?"

"The only part that didn't appeal to me last night was the water."

"You were wonderful," she said, and he questioned her with a look. "Today. Your music. You play beautifully, and you sing like—"

"Thanks." He swung his jacket down from his shoulder. "It's a good song."

"It's a *lovely* song. Perfect. I don't think I've heard it before."

"Aw, c'mon. You gotta love those Dixie Chicks. I had to change a couple of words to make it work."

"You made it yours. *Theirs.* Annie's and Zach's. That'll be their song now." Feeling a sudden chill, she hugged herself and rubbed her bare upper arms.

"What a gift, Hank. That's something they'll take with them throughout their journey together. *Their song.*"

"You're layin' it on a little thick, there, Sally," he teased as he laid his jacket over her shoulders.

"Never. I'm no gusher. If anything, that was an understatement. My little sister just got married, Hank. If I could sing, I'd be..." She adjusted the jacket and began to sway. "You know what? I can dance." She did a tiny two-step, added a slow twirl, and then a more enthusiastic two-step and a spin. "I can dance. *I can...*"

She lost the twinkle in her toes, stumbled, and landed in a hoop made of two strong arms.

"Oops. I tend to be a little clumsy when I get excited. All I need is a strong partner." She copped a feel of his working-man's biceps as she steadied herself and eased up on him, catching a knowing look beneath the brim of his hat. He thought it a pratfall.

She smiled. "How about it?"

He took his time about tilting her upright, the corner of his mouth twitching. "How about I do the singin' and you do the dancin'?"

"They didn't set this up very well. The best man is married. What fun is that for a maid of honor?"

He bent to retrieve his jacket from the grass. "What kind of fun are you looking for?"

"The loosen-your-tie-and-kick-your-shoes-off kind. How about you?"

"If I start taking more clothes off, the party's over."

He draped his jacket over her shoulders again. "I'll settle for a good meal and a little music."

"Ah, the quiet type. A challenge is always fun." She linked arms with him and made a sweeping gesture toward the lodge. "Shall we? Dinner's coming up soon. Right now the bar is open and the drinks are free."

"Free drinks would take away any challenge if I didn't have this booze-sniffin' bitch with me." The dog whined and perked her ears. "See? Phoebe don't miss a trick. No way am I goin' near any open bar, so just save me a seat at the dinner table."

"I've already arranged the place cards. You're next to me on the wagon." She had him walking now. Ambling. She was in no hurry. "Have you thought about my suggestion?"

"What suggestion?"

"Think of it as sort of a working vacation. Not hard labor, mind you. More like backup. Hang out with Hoolie and me. We can be quite entertaining. And according to Zach, you're unattached and somewhat flexible in your schedule." She looked up and gave a perfunctory smile. "I asked."

"Why would you do that?"

"Filling out your résumé. I didn't tell him you were thinking about applying for the job. So far, this is just between you and me."

"You're serious."

"Of course I'm serious. I want my sister's wedding to be perfect, and the perfect wedding includes a fabulous honeymoon." She gave his arm what she hoped felt like a winning squeeze. "I don't know what your somewhat flexible schedule looks like for the next few weeks, but you wouldn't have to miss any rodeos. Come and go as you please, but stow your gear with us for a while. That way there's another man around, and the honeymooners have nothing to worry about."

"What about the man? Should I be worried?"

"You don't strike me as a worrier."

"Long as I'm not hangin' with troublemakers, I got nothin' to worry about."

"No worries, then." She laughed. "I really don't make trouble. I fall into it sometimes, but who doesn't?" She looked up. "You?"

"Not lately."

"Maybe you need a little adventure in your life, Hank. Get out there, you know? Try new things. New people. I like to get while the gettin's good, but I'm always careful. You gotta be careful with the good stuff, right? Good people, good ideas, good times—there's a certain balance. A little daring goes a long way with a lot of careful." She wagged an instructive finger. "If we had an emergency, we'd call you."

"There's nobody crazier than Zach Beaudry when it comes to risking his neck, and you can tell him I said so."

"And he'll say he's changed." She stopped, turned, blocked his progress. "Will you think about it? What's three weeks?"

"How much time do I have to think about it?"

"About three hours." She pulled his jacket in tighter. "Do you have horses? I could pay you in horses. You know, the Indian way."

"Yeah, I know the Indian way. But you're talkin' Sally's way, and I'm goin' Hank's way. Nice try, though." He smiled. "I do like the way you swim."

"Dance with me tonight, and I'll swim with you later."

"For me, that's a whole lotta daring and not much careful." He slipped his arm around her shoulders. "Be damned if I'm not tempted to jump in."

Hank generally steered clear of big parties, but the Beaudry wedding was turning out to be a pretty good time. With beef for dinner and the prospect of Sally for dessert, he was happy to loosen his belt now and put his boots under her bed later. She hadn't been kidding about arranging the place cards. She'd given up her seat at the bride's table, supposedly so the best man could sit with his wife. She'd grabbed Hilda Beaudry and nodded toward Hoolie and Hank, who'd claimed a table on the sidelines and started in on the bread basket. It was a good setup. Hank wouldn't presume to guess where Hoolie pictured parking his boots tonight, but he secretly wished the old man whatever he could score. Hilda was definitely enjoying the company.

"It's too bad you can't dance tonight, Hoolie," Hilda said, genuinely grieved.

Hoolie checked all his pockets. "Too many hidey-holes in this monkey suit. I don't know where my pocket knife went to. You got one on you, Hank? I'm gonna cut this damn thing off."

"No nudity here, Hoolie." Sally winked at Hank. "Wait till we're back in camp."

"Is that where you're hiding all the Double D's?" Hank scanned the room. "'Cause I ain't seein' any in this crowd."

"I'm talkin' about this mummy's boot I got on my foot," Hoolie grumbled.

"How long you had it on?" Hank asked.

"About a month."

"About a week," Sally said.

"Sorry, Hoolie. You got a ways to go."

"I broke a wing before. Twice." Hoolie flapped his folded arm. "But never a leg. Sure cramps a guy's style."

"I'll request the Funky Chicken," Hilda promised. "When the mother of the groom and the father of the bride are both unattached, they get one of those spotlight dances. Right, Sally?"

"Absolutely. We make our own rules. Don't we, Hoolie? I think I might have found us a sitter." She flashed Hank a smile. "Hank's almost convinced."

"What kind of a sitter?" Hoolie scowled.

"The kind who looks like he can keep the mice at bay while the cats go play. Hank's perfect, so help me put him over the edge." She laid her hand on Hank's shoulder and crooned, "Come on out to the big Double D, where the horses run wild and the cowboys live free."

Hank chuckled. "Yeah, that's gonna do it."

"Hell, yeah, we want those kids to have their honeymoon." Hoolie leaned closer to Hank. "You like horses?"

"He's a farrier," Sally said.

"Thought you was an MA or a PD or some kind of code for junior doctor."

"PA," Hank said. "Physician's assistant."

"For people, right? And you can shoe horses besides?" Hoolie grinned. "Yeah, you need to come see our place. You got some time? Say about—"

"Three weeks? They don't trust you to mind the store either, Hoolie?" Hank asked.

"They would if I hadn't gone and—"

Sally whapped Hoolie in the chest and nodded toward a paunchy silhouette in an oversized straw hat looming in the doorway to the dining room. "What's he doing here?"

Hoolie peered, squinted. "Don't ask me."

"Annie thought about inviting the Tutans. Double D diplomacy, she said, but after the last stunt he pulled—I know damn well it was him—I said it was him or me." Sally's hand found Hank's forearm again, but like Hoolie, he was zeroed in on the uninvited guest. "He cut our fence," she was saying. "We keep the old horses in a separate pasture, and Tutan cut the fence. He said he didn't, but it was definitely cut, and that's how Hoolie broke his ankle."

"That was my own damn fault."

"We have special fencing separating the young horses from the retirees and the convalescents. Those horses don't get through a four-strand fence without help." Sally slid her chair back. "I'm sure it was a trap. I don't know if it was set for the horses or for you, but I know he did it to cause us trouble. And he's about to get his."

"Hold on, girl." Hoolie's chair legs scraped the floor. "Not now."

"I don't want him anywhere near Annie's wedding."

"C'mon." Hank was the first one to his feet. "This is my kind of fun. Don't worry, Hoolie. We'll keep it civil." He smiled as he helped Sally with her chair. "But there's nothing wrong with showin' a little claw."

Tutan. The name ping-ponged within the walls of Hank's head as he took in the face for the first time. He kept pace with Sally, who had a point to make with every deliberate step. *No hurry. I'm in charge here.* His admiration for the woman's style grew with every moment he spent with her. And now, here was Dan Tutan. Her lease challenger. His father's leash holder. *Mr. Tutan.*

"We're on our way to Rapid City, thought we'd stop in and offer our best wishes. Did you get our gift?"

"We did. Thanks, but you really shouldn't have."

No *hello*, no *go to hell*. The way Sally was bristling and the man was posturing, Hank expected a little snarling. He was disappointed.

"We've been neighbors a long time, Sally." The man with the round, red face adjusted his hat, hitched up his pants, and finally folded his arms over his barrel chest. "We figured our invitation got lost in the mail."

"Annie wanted to keep it small. Family and close friends."

He eyed Hank. "Close friends?"

"Hank Night Horse." No handshake. A nod and a name were more than enough. "I've known Zach a long time."

"Night Horse." Tutan went snake eyed. "I had a guy by that name working for me years ago. Any relation to you?"

Keep looking, Mr. Tutan. "Where was he from?"

"I don't think he was from around here. Coulda been Montana. Isn't that where Beaudry's from?"

"Yeah, it is."

"I like that Crow Indian country up there. Real pretty. Is that where you're from?"

"Nope." *Crow country is Crow country.* "But Night Horse is a common name. Kinda like Drexler and Tutan."

"That guy that worked for me…there's something…" He kept staring, the rude bastard. But he shook his head. "No, if I remember right, he was shaped more like me." He patted his belly and laughed. "And he was a good hand. Except when he got to drinking. Fell off the wagon and got himself killed somehow. Hard to tell by the time his body was found, but they thought he might've been out hunting. That's one sport you don't want to mix with too much Everclear." He shook his head. "Tragic."

"Sounds like it." Hank stared dispassionately, kept his tone tame and his fists tucked into his elbows.

"Maybe that wasn't his name. Pretty sure it was some kinda Horse." Tutan turned to Sally. "You're looking fit. Some new kind of—"

"I'm doing well, thanks. *Very* well."

"Good. Good to hear." He tried to peer past Sally, but it was Hoolie who limped into view. "Good man, Hoolihan," Tutan enthused. "There's sure no keeping you down. Where's the bride? I just want to give her my best. I've known these girls most of their lives, and I want little Annie to know that the Tutans wish her well."

"She's on a tight schedule," Hank said. "We'll tell her you stopped in."

"This time tomorrow I guess the happy couple will be off on a nice honeymoon."

"That's the main reason I'm here." Hank drew a deep breath, steadying himself. "Zach and Annie won't have a thing to worry about. I'll be keepin' these two in line."

"You're gonna have your hands full, son." Tutan threaded his thumbs under his belly roll and over his belt as he moved in on Sally. "Tell your sister I wish her well. She and Beaudry would do well to get out of this crazy horse thing you've got going and live their lives. You and your wild ideas. You're just trying to keep your sister from leaving you without—"

Hank caught Sally in time to save Tutan from what undoubtedly would have been a nice right hook if she'd followed through.

Backpedaling, Tutan wagged his finger. "Your father's rolling over in his grave over what you've done to the Double D, Sally."

"This is a private party, Tutan," Hoolie said.

Tutan's angry gaze didn't waver. "Hell, girl, I'm sorry for all your troubles, but I ain't rollin' over. I've got a *real* ranch to run."

"Let me go," Sally grumbled as Tutan turned on his heel and stomped across the lobby.

Hank eased up, but he wasn't letting go until Tutan was out the door. "Marriage and murder are too much for one day."

She drew herself up and challenged him with a look. "You're the one who suggested showing some claw."

"A *little*."

"Night Horse," she said quietly. "He said the man worked for him."

"And you heard my answer."

"What I heard was…" She took his warning from his eyes. "Did you mean it? About helping out?"

"Actually, I was just sayin' it to help out, but then he went and called me *son*." He gave a curt nod. "Yeah, if it'll make a difference, I'll stay."

"Let's go tell the bride and groom." She grabbed his hand. "You're just full of great gifts. They'll be calling you Santa Claus."

"You might be callin' me Scrooge. You kids won't be having any parties with me in charge."

"Actually…" She leaned in close, and he had half a mind to take that flower out of her hair so he could smell only Sally. She was giving him those eyes again, full of fireworks and mischief. "I'm looking forward to that part about the party being over."

He laughed. "You're the damnedest woman I ever met."

"Only when I'm at my best."

"Sally!" Glistening with bride shine, Annie burst on the scene, brushing Hank's arm as she reached for her sister. "Are you okay? Somebody said…"

"Everything's okay. Look. Not a scratch on me, and Tutan got off easy. Come with me to the bathroom." Sally put her unscratched arm around her sister's shoulders and wheeled her in the opposite direction. "I gotta go talk her down," she told Hank in parting. "Keep the big surprise under your hat."

For how long? Hank wondered as he watched the Drexlers head for the women's sanctuary. He'd be walking around with a bombshell under his hat until somebody took the detonator out of his mouth by whispering Thanks, Hank, but you won't be needed after all.

"It was nothing." Sally snatched a tissue from the box beside the sink and used it to dab a lipstick smudge from her sister's cheek. "Tutan said he was on his way to Rapid City and just stopped in to make sure you got his gift. Don't open it. It's probably some kind of curse on your firstborn."

"Did you put any scratches on him?"

"I came so close. If Hank hadn't interfered…"

"Then what?" Annie prompted. But before Sally's very eyes, the question of *what* took a mental backseat to the *who*. Annie smiled. "*Hank*. Zach was right. He said you two would hit it off."

"I'd like to see more of him." At least as much as he'd seen of her. Feeling good, looking fine—she glanced at herself in the mirror, just to make sure, yes—for now and however much longer, she would do her best to see and know, give and take with a man, *this* man.

She raised a cautionary finger. "Remember, Annie, I tell *who* I want, *when* and *if* I want. And for right now, I'm as healthy as you are. You haven't said anything, have you?"

"I hardly know the man."

Sally nodded. "I would have hit him."

"Hank?"

"No, Tutan. It would have felt *so good*. But Hank held me back." She smiled. "And that felt even better."

Annie gave her that what-are-you-up-to? look. She always recognized the signs. "You didn't sign us up for one of those reality shows, did you?"

"You mean like 'My Big Fat Redneck Wedding'?" Sally snapped her fingers. "Hey, we could have gotten some publicity for the sanctuary. I wish I'd thought of that." She laughed. "Just kidding."

"Seriously, you're having a good time?"

"I'm gonna dance my shoes off tonight, little sister." Sally fussed with Annie's golden curls. "You're so beautiful."

"You're giving me that look. What else have you got up your sleeve?"

"Are you kidding? I can barely hide my boobs in this dress." Sally winked. She could barely contain herself. "It's no wonder you're a teacher—you read me like a book. I do have a little surprise for you. I think. I hope. Like you said, we hardly know the man."

"Another song?"

"You want another song?" Sally leaned closer to the mirror and adjusted her décolleté. "I'll see what I can do."

Hank sang "Can I Have This Dance?" for Zach and Ann Beaudry, who waltzed alone in the spotlight, surrounded by family and friends smiling in the dark. Beautiful people. Sally's throat tingled. Her eyes smarted with happy tears. Her heart was fuller than she could have imagined in the days before the wedding, when her only sister was still a bride-to-be and Hank Night Horse was simply a name on a list. She wanted to catch the moment and slip it into a magic bottle, preserve it in all its sensory glory for a time when her senses would not serve and she would turn to memory.

Hank left the cheers and applause to the bride and groom and the music for the wedding party dance to the DJ. Sally smiled as the best man reported for duty, but by the time she was able to get a good look past Sam's nicely tailored shoulder, her private man of the hour had disappeared. She added his modesty to the growing list of his irresistible qualities and committed herself to leaving him alone for a few minutes.

But when she escaped to the terrace, her commitment fell by the wayside at the sight of the guitar leaning against the balcony along with the man seated on the top rail. A sinking feeling in her legs urged her to pull him down before he fell backward, but she fought her foolishness with a slow, deep breath. Strong sensation was good, even the silly, sinking kind. Anything was better than numbness, which would be slinking back sooner or later along with whatever other anomalies the erratic disease lurking in her body had in store. She threw back her shoulders and walked the planks, taking care not to turn an ankle over the kitten heels that had been her compromise to the killer spikes she'd longed to wear just this once and the safe flats Annie had tried to talk her into.

He watched her. He didn't smile much, this man with the breathtaking voice, but as the bright lights and music fell away from the starry night, he summoned her with his steady gaze.

"What took you so long?" he asked quietly.

"I've danced with Sam and his boy, Jimmy. I've danced with Zach. I've even danced with their mother. But I have not danced with you. Do you always sing and run?"

"Yep."

"If I didn't know better, I might have gone looking for you at the bar."

"But you do know better."

"I do." She stood close enough to touch him, but she laid her hand on the railing and reveled in the feel of the wood and the wanting. "You've been with Phoebe?"

"Took her for a walk. Had to keep her on a tight leash when some guy came along with something that looked like a giant poodle. Phoebe was ready to tear into that thing."

"Blessed are the peacemakers."

"You're right." He came down from the railing like a cat, languidly stretching one long leg at a time, pulled her to him with one arm, took her free hand and tucked it against his chest. "We should dance."

"Mmm-hmm. This is nice." She swayed in his arms, brushing against him just enough to incite sweet shivers. "Peaceful, but not still."

"If I didn't know better, I'd say we'd met before."

"In another life?"

"How many do you have?"

"Three at least, maybe more. But I'm sure this is the only one I've met you in."

He laughed. He thought she was joking.

"*So far,*" she said, and he drew her closer. She rested her head on his shoulder and inhaled his zesty scent, wondering what he tasted like and how soon she would find out. "But I know what you mean. It feels like we needed no introduction."

"It was a jaw-dropping introduction. Maybe it wasn't necessary, but I sure wouldn't trade it for a handshake."

"You barged in on the life behind door number one. Good choice."

"Phoebe has good instincts."

If anyone but her sister had interrupted, Sally would have hissed mightily.

"Is this a private party?" Annie ventured.

Sally peeked around Hank's shoulder and smiled.

"Not if we can wangle a private audience with the bride and groom." She gave Hank's hand a quick squeeze. "We have a proposition for you."

Zach laughed. "I told you somebody was getting propositioned."

"Tell them, Hank." Sally flashed him a smile, but he wouldn't buy in that far. She turned the smile on her sister. "You two are going on that honeymoon."

"Maybe this fall," Ann said. "Or this winter, or—"

"Maybe *this week*. I ran a little contest, and Hank won himself an all-expenses-paid vacation at the Double D Dude Ranch."

"Wait a minute," Hank said. Sally held her breath. "I thought you ran a little want ad, and I got *hired*."

Sally exhaled a laugh, inhaled relief. "You didn't qualify for the job, but all applicants were automatically entered into the drawing for a vacation, and you're our winner."

"What'd I tell you, Horse?" Zach clapped his hand on his friend's shoulder. "You come to my wedding, you're bound to get lucky."

"Sally, you didn't." Ann's eyes sparkled. She was on top of the world, but she would gladly make room for her sister.

"Didn't what? Award the grand prize already? He's not *that* lucky." Sally glanced askance, giving Hank a coy smile. "But the winner of the vacation may become eligible for—"

"No, no, no," Ann said. "It's the second-sweetest offer I've heard all day, but we can't go halfway around the world and leave Hank to take care of things at the Double D. It's way too much to ask. He has places to go and things to do."

"Which is why I'll be the one taking care of things at the Double D. All Hank has to take care of is your peace of mind. And he's happy to do that." Sally linked arms with Hank. He wasn't going anywhere anytime soon. "Right, Hank?"

"Absolutely. You two lovebirds enjoy yourselves. I'll stand guard over the nest while you're gone."

"Oh, Hank, we really appreciate the offer, but with—"

"But nothing," Sally said. "It's perfect."

"I have a couple of commitments to work around, but Sally's been telling me about the program you're running, and I'm interested. I can use a little—" Hank slid Sally a conspiratorial glance. "—diversion."

"Can we trust these two?" Ann asked her new husband.

"I can vouch for Hank. Salt of the earth. Even if we had eggs in the nest, I'd trust him."

"Nobody's vouched for *you* yet," the bride reminded her sister. She looked up at Zach. "Is it safe to leave the salt of the earth with a shaker that doesn't always have her head screwed on straight?"

"I do like to shake things up," Sally said. She

glanced up at Hank. "I used to be a mover, too, but that's a lot of work."

"I don't shake easy," he told her.

"Hank's the right man for the job," Zach said. "I'd even trust him with Zelda."

"You hear that?" Sally asked Ann. "If Zach's willing to leave the keys to his precious pickup in Hank's hands, you know your sister is safe."

"Can we still do it? I mean, we canceled the reservations, but we still have the tickets." Ann turned to Hank. "I don't travel that much, and I would've been happy with an extra night right here in the Hills, but Sam gave us this trip to Australia. *Australia.* I've always wanted to…"

"You go, Mrs. Beaudry," Hank said. "Live the dream."

"I owe you, man."

"Damn straight, cowboy." Hank waved a cautionary finger at the groom, but his warning was for the bride. "I don't ever wanna see this guy on my exam table again."

"That makes two of us. But Sally—"

"Best behavior," Sally promised. "Pinky swear."

Chapter Three

Hank had never considered himself to be a cowboy, but he was a horseman. He owned two mares, pastured them at what was now really his brother Greg's place up north, just across the state line. Hank also owned some of the land, but Greg's cattle used it. All Hank asked in return was a room, a mailing address and a place to keep a few horses. He didn't take up much space.

Hank was no breeder or fancier, wasn't out to acquire pedigrees or trophies. He'd rescued the two mares from a farm foreclosure. They'd been bony and riddled with parasites, about as sad eyed and desperate as the old man who was losing all he had and looking for somebody, *any*body with a heart to take in the last of his stock. Hank had even offered to adopt the farmer, but his niece had shown up for that end of the rescue. Wormed, fed up, trimmed up and turned out on Dakota grass, the two mares had turned out to be pretty nice. Not the best of his rescues—he'd taken in a sweet-tempered colt that had gone to a couple looking for a friend for their autistic child—but they would make good saddle horses if he ever found the time to work with them.

Three hundred miles northeast of the Hilltop Lodge, Hank checked in at home and took care of his personal business. The next day he drove nearly the same distance due south to the Double D. Not that he was in a killing hurry to start his "vacation"—a vacation for Hank would have meant stringing together a few nights in what he loosely termed his own bed—but he had promises to keep and curiosity to satisfy. He cared a lot about his friend, Zach Beaudry. He'd heard a lot about the Double D. He'd thought a lot about Sally Drexler. He had a bad feeling about her neighbor. It all added up to a sense of purpose, and Hank Night Horse was a man of purpose.

He called ahead to make sure he knew where he was going once he ran out of map markings. The two-story farmhouse was off the state highway at the end of about three miles of sparsely graveled road. He found Sally waiting for him on the sprawling covered porch. She came down the steps to greet him.

"Hey, Phoebe."

Okay, so she greeted his dog first. Unlike Hank, Phoebe was not above making a slobbering fool of herself.

"You just missed the honeymooners," Sally told him, her eyes unmistakably alight for him.

"You got time for TV?" He wasn't above grinning.

"I've always got time for a comedian." She took a hands-on-hips stance and gave his pickup with its custom long-box cap an appreciative once-over. The sleek, slide-in cargo box was outfitted for his business and his gypsy lifestyle. "You must have done just about what the newlyweds did. Grabbed your gear and run. Of course, they had a plane to catch. Are you hungry? Tired? Ready to rock 'n' roll?"

"I'll do anything that doesn't involve sitting."

She raised her brow. "Interested in reclining?"

"If I do that, I'm liable to be out for a while."

"Then let's walk and talk before we eat, drink and be merry." She gave a come-on gesture. "I'll show you around."

Her walk wasn't quite as smooth as her talk. He'd noticed it before, but it was so subtle, he'd dismissed it as another of her quirks. Sally wasn't your standard model female in any way, shape or form. She was special. Easy to follow, hard to figure, no doubt heavy on the upkeep.

Hardly the best fit for Hank Night Horse. He was an

ordinary man who talked with a straight tongue and tried to walk a straight line. He understood most people—once you figured out what they wanted, for better or worse they were generally predictable—but Sally was like a horse he'd ridden for an elderly neighbor when he was a kid. Four out of five days the beautiful Arabian was smart, spirited, smooth-gaited, a dream to ride. But on the fifth day she'd likely take off with him and run like a hellcat until they hit some kind of a wall. She was four-fifths dream and one-fifth damned, but she was special. And four days out of five, she sure was fun to play with.

He wasn't sure about the hitch in Sally's gait. It was slight and oddly sporadic. An old injury wouldn't seem to explain it, and maybe there was no explanation. Maybe it was just Sally.

They entered the machine shed through a side door, which was propped open for ventilation. Hoolie looked up from a workbench and then slid off the stool before he remembered he wasn't going anywhere without his crutch.

He grinned anyway and reached for Hank's handshake. "Did you bring all the tools of your trades? My saddle horse could use corrective shoes, and I'll pay you to take this damn mummy boot off my hoof."

"Like I told you before, you take that off too soon, you'll pay dearly. Your horse is a different story. My pickup is a blacksmith shop on wheels. Phoebe!" The dog was headed for the door.

"Does she get along with other dogs?" Sally asked.

"Sure does. She's around dogs all the time."

A warning growl sounded outside the door.

"Well, that makes one of them," Hoolie said ominously as a black-and-white shepherd slunk across the threshold, teeth bared.

"Baby!"

Sally bolted for the door, but she fell flat on her face before she got there. Tripped over her own feet like one of the TV comedians she'd claimed she always had time for. She was doing a shaky push-up on the concrete by the time Hank got to her. She tried to wave him off, her attention fixed on the dogs.

Hoolie came on strong once he had his crutch in place. "Here, you dogs, you want a piece o' me?"

The clamor settled into a war of whines, both bitches determined to get in the last whimper as Hoolie and his crutch prevailed.

Hank found himself down on one knee beside a woman who was on her way up. "You okay?"

"Yes! Yes, of course." She laughed as she braced her hand on his shoulder. "Totally wasn't ready for that. Scared me."

"They're okay," Hoolie called out. "Phoebe wants to play. Baby wants to lay down a few rules first."

"I'll give 'em some rules," Hank grumbled, discomfited by the loss of his dignity and his own confusion as to where it had gone.

Sally laughed again. "What are you, the Dog Whisperer?"

"I'm the alpha." He signaled Phoebe to stay put while the shepherd took a fallback position. "You got any other dogs around here?" he asked Sally.

"Baby's an only dog."

"That's her problem. We'll fix it, though. We'll teach her some manners. Won't we, Phoeb?" Hank patted the dog's silky head. "Scared you, huh?"

"It sure startled me." Sally twisted her arm for a look at her skinned elbow. "I didn't want to lose you over a dogfight. You've probably noticed I can be kind of a klutz sometimes. Two left feet." She gave a perfunctory smile. "Except when I dance."

"You stick to dancing and leave us to referee the dogs."

"Only if you'll dance with me, Henry." She was giving him that too cute look. "Do you know that song? You're supposed to say, *Okay, Baby.*"

Hank shook his head. "Nobody calls me Henry."

"That's your real name, isn't it?" She flashed a smile at Hoolie. "Henry's a fine name."

"*No*body calls me Henry."

"Ah, the soft underbelly. Our guardian is ticklish, Hoolie."

"I know the feeling," Hoolie said.

"I can handle a dogfight, but that name is a deal breaker."

"Duly noted." Sally slid a glance at Hoolie, who chuckled.

"Okay, now aren't you supposed to have some wild horses around here somewhere?"

"That's the rumor. But first, the tour." She gave an after-you gesture. "Please follow the silk thread."

Hank raised his brow and responded in kind. He knew her game. She was like his patients on the rodeo circuit— too stubborn to say they were hurt, so you didn't ask. You watched how they moved. *If* they'd let you.

"No go?" She grabbed his arm and coaxed him by her side. "All right, then, when you're ready to put your road-weary butt in a saddle, I'll show you horses, Henry. *Hank.*"

"You're askin' for it, woman."

"For what?" She met his loaded look with a coy smile. "Oh, no. I'm just hackin' on you. Make no mistake, when it comes to serious matters, I don't fool around." She glanced away. "Well, I do, but I don't ask. Do you?"

What he didn't do was answer foolish questions.

By the time he'd seen the outbuildings—shop, machine shed, barn, loafing shed, grain bins, bunk house—the suggestion of food held considerable appeal. He was impressed with what he'd seen so far. It was a nice layout, but the cattle operation was a shadow of what it had been in its heyday, two generations ago. According to Hank's tour guide, the Double D ran a small herd of cattle, partly to satisfy state requirements to claim agricultural status and partly for income. But the ranch's main enterprise was the wild-horse sanctuary, and it was decidedly nonprofit. An unusual concept for a third-generation rancher, but Sally Drexler was an unusual rancher. Hank looked forward to seeing the horses.

After his stomach stopped growling.

He hit the front steps heavily to cover the noise as he headed for the door behind Sally, but the twinkle in her eyes let him know she wasn't deaf. Embarrassing. He didn't like to give anything away unintentionally. Not even the fact that he hadn't taken time to eat anything before he left home.

Beset by the aroma of juicy beef, his stomach spoke up again as he followed her in the house while Phoebe protested having the door shut in her face.

"She can come in, as long as she's okay around cats," Sally said. "Sounds like she's hungry. We usually don't eat supper around here until pretty late, but we never keep the critters waiting."

"Something smells good." He stood like a maypole while Sally circled around him. "Enough to eat." He watched her let Phoebe in. "Right now."

She turned one of her bright-eyed smiles on him. "Right now?"

"Be glad to help you get it on."

"Would you?"

"On the table."

"I've always wanted to try that," she told him over her shoulder as she led the way through foodless territory. "But let's eat first."

Willing as he was, he didn't have to help much. He was a straight shooter, and she was a woman who loved to tease. She'd had supper simmering in a Crock-Pot, ready to dish up anytime. She put him to slicing bread and filling water glasses while she washed salad greens. Hoolie came in the back door all slicked down and washed up precisely at five-fifteen.

Pretty late, my ass.

Pretty tasty. Pretty entertaining. Pretty woman. Maybe he could get used to a little teasing.

"How much of the Double D can you reach on wheels?" Hank asked as he sipped his coffee. "You use ATVs?"

"Hell, no," Hoolie said. "Too damn noisy. This is a ranch, not a playground."

"I'm with you on that score." And he'd told his brother as much last night when Greg had shown off a picture of the one he wanted. A kid's toy, Hank had said.

"We can cover a lot of ground in a pickup, but there's places we don't go except on horseback."

"We have some totally pristine grassland here," Sally said. "Some of it is pretty remote."

"I'll stow my gear in the bunkhouse, and then maybe we could all take a little pickup ride," Hank suggested. "Give me a feel for what's out there while it's still light."

"We can do that." Sally sounded hesitant. "But we have a room for you here in the house."

"I'm fine with the bunkhouse."

"We get kids out here sometimes helpin' out. Volunteers come and go. You'll be better off in the house." Hoolie shrugged. "I snore."

"We're hoping to add on to the bunkhouse to give Hoolie more privacy." Sally and Hoolie exchanged looks. "Definitely on the to-do list."

"Definitely," Hoolie said. "Sally's used to having Annie around. And Zach, too, since he come along. We don't want Sally rattlin' around here alone at night."

"She could get into trouble?" Hank set his cup down. "Hell, whatever works. I just figured…"

"It's a big house," Hoolie said. "And you're a guest more than anything. I'm the hired man."

Hank looked at Sally. He had something she wanted, and she'd decided it was hers for the taking. She'd try to tease it out of him, would she? He gave a suggestive smile. *Game on, woman. Your house, my play.*

"Do *you* snore?" he asked her.

"I've never had any complaints."

Hoolie took Sally's unspoken hint and begged off the after-supper tour. "I'll let you take my pickup." He offered Hank two keys and a metal Road Runner trinket on a key ring.

Ignoring the handoff, Hank nodded at Sally. "She's giving the tour."

"This thing he offers is a great honor," Sally quipped, B-movie style. "To refuse would be an insult."

"She's a 1968 C10," Hoolie boasted. "She's a great little go-fer pickup. Short box with a six-pony engine. Overhauled her myself."

"Classic," Hank said appreciatively. "My dad had one when I was a kid. Got her used, ran her into the ground. He was on the road a lot."

"Don't know how many times the odometer's turned over on this one, but she runs like a top. You gotta try 'er out."

"My pleasure."

Watching Hank handle the big steering wheel and palm the knob on the gearshift was Sally's pleasure. She'd stopped driving altogether after proving she really could hit the broad side of the barn. It was the first time she'd lost all feeling in her right leg, the one that gave her the most trouble. She'd been backing up to the barn with a load of mineral blocks when suddenly the leg was gone. Might as well have been lopped off at the hip. By the time she'd moved the dead weight by hand, her tailgate had smashed through the tack-room wall.

The damage to the barn had been easy to repair. Her

pickup, like her pride, had become an early victim of her unpredictable body. But her independence had begun to erode that day, and with it went bits of confidence. Dealing with the disease wasn't as difficult as plugging up holes in her spirit. During bad times she'd start springing holes right and left, and she could feel herself draining away. She'd learned to take advantage of the very thing that made MS so cruel—its capricious nature. When the symptoms ebbed, she dammed up all her leaks and charged ahead, full speed, total Sally. She took pleasure in the little things, like the way it felt to get up and walk whenever the spirit moved her, the feel of water lapping against bare skin, the smell of a summer night and the look of a man's hands taking charge.

Phoebe was sitting pretty in the pickup box behind the back window, her blond ears flapping in the breeze. They plied the fence line at a leisurely pace, following tire tracks worn in the sod. Sally pointed out the "geriatric bachelor band" grazing in a shallow draw. They were too old for the adoption program, and some of them had spent years in holding facilities—essentially feedlot conditions—before finding a home at the Double D. Heads bobbed, ears perked at the sound of the engine, and they moved as one, like a school of fish.

"They have no use for us, especially this time of year," she said with a smile. "Which means we're doing something right." She nodded for a swing to the west, punched the glove-compartment button and felt around for the binoculars. "From the top of that hill we might get a look at some of the two-year-olds. There are some beauties in that bunch. Do you like Spanish Mustangs?"

He swung the big steering wheel. "I don't see too many."

"They don't come shoe shopping?"

"I work mostly rodeos, so I see a lot of quarter horses." The engine growled as he downshifted for the hill. "I did shoe a couple of mustangs at an endurance ride last fall. They had real pretty feet."

"We need to interest more people in adopting these horses. The BLM had an auction out in Wyoming last month and sold less than half the number they projected. If they don't find any more takers and we can't make room for them, some of them will end up..." She glimpsed movement below the hill and to the right, but she had to turn her head to see what it was. Her right eye was going out on her again. *Damn.* "Look!" She pushed the binoculars against his arm. "Stop! Hurry, before they get away."

"Look, stop, hurry?" He complied, chuckling. "How about hurry, stop, look? Or—"

"Shh!" She tapped him with the binoculars again, and he took them and focused. "How many? Can you tell?"

"Eight. Nine."

"See any you like?"

"Nice red roan. Three buckskins. Aw, man, would you look at that bay."

He offered her a turn with the binoculars, but she shook them off. "I can't use those things. But I know which one you mean. He looks just like his daddy. Fabulous Spanish Sulphur Mustang stallion we call Don Quixote." She nodded as he put the binoculars up to his face again. *Stop, take a look, really see.* "Give that boy another year, and you'd have yourself an endurance racer, a cutting horse, whatever your pleasure."

"You won't have any trouble finding him a good home." He glanced at her. "If you're having trouble with numbers, show me what's left after the next auction."

"We can usually place a few more with special programs. Police units, military, youth programs, even prisons."

"After all's said and done, show me what's left. Never met a horse I didn't like." He handed her the binoculars. "I'd sure like to see that bay up close."

"You will. They're getting cut this week."

"All of them?"

"Only the ones with balls. If you like the bay when you see him up close, he could be spared." She smiled at him as she snapped the glove compartment shut. "Which puts his balls in your court."

"Damn." He chuckled as he lifted his hand to the key in the ignition.

"He'd make a wonderful stud." She stayed his hand

with hers and slid to the middle of the bench seat. "This is my favorite time of day. Between sunset and dusk. Late meadowlarks, early crickets."

He said nothing. The enigmatic look in his eyes wasn't what she expected. Maybe she'd misread his signals. Maybe her receptors were on the blink. Life's ultimate joke. Just when she was getting the *go* light on all major systems except her troublesome right eye, which wasn't a major system at the moment.

She would not take this lying down.

Who was she kidding? She'd take him any way she could get him, but in a small pickup, lying down wasn't gonna happen.

Alternatives?

"Did you ever go parking in your father's C10?" she asked.

"He was dead and the pickup was gone by the time I started meetin' up with girls after sunset."

"Where did you meet them?"

"Down by the river. You're fifteen and you get a chance to be with a girl, you're not lookin' to take the high ground."

"Fifteen?"

"Late bloomer." He moved the seat back as far as it would go and put his arm around her. "I like this time of day, too, Sally."

He leaned over her slowly, fingers in her hair, thumb grazing her cheek, lips moistened and parted just enough to make hers quiver on the cusp of his kiss. He made her feel dear and delicate, and she was having none of it. She slipped her arm around his neck and answered his sweet approach with her spicy reception. She was no weak-kneed quiverer. She could match him slam for bam and thank you, man. She didn't need coddling, and she told him as much with a heat-seeking kiss.

The catch in his breath pleased her. The new-found need in his kiss thrilled her. She answered in kind, kissing him like there was no time like the present. Because there wasn't. Deep, caring kisses like his were rare. She drew a breath full of the salty taste and sexy scent of him and grazed his chest with her breasts. They drew taut within her clothing. She pushed her fingers through his hair, curled them and rubbed it against the center of her palm. She would fill her senses with him while she could, because she could. She slipped her free hand between them, found his belly, hard and flat as his belt buckle. She took the measure of both.

He nuzzled the side of her neck and groaned. "I'm not fifteen anymore," he whispered. "I can wait."

"Why would you? I'm not a girl."

He raised his head and smiled at her. "In this light you could be. Young and scared. A little confused, maybe."

She frowned. "But since I'm none of those things…"

"I don't know that." He caressed her face with the backs of his fingers. "Who said you could call all the shots?"

"Is there something wrong with me?" She swallowed hard. "I mean, something you don't like?"

"Uh-uh. Everything looks just right."

"Looks can deceive." She dragged her fingers from his belt to his zipper. "But this feels right."

"You don't wanna believe that guy." He moved his hips just enough to let her know that there was nothing wrong with him, either. "No matter what the question, he's only got one answer."

"He's honest," she whispered. "Stands up for what he believes in."

He kissed her again, so fully and thoroughly that the taste of his lips and the darting of his tongue, the strength of his arms and the sharp intake of his breath satisfied all her wishes. She had feeling in every part of her body. She didn't want it to go away, not one tingle, not one spark, and she reached around him and held him the way he held her. Maybe more so. Maybe harder and stronger and more desirous of him than he could possibly be of her, but she was honest. Her embrace was true to what she felt, and feeling was everything.

"Easy," he whispered, and she realized she had sounded some sort of alarm, made some desperate little noise. "You okay?"

She nodded. Laughed a little. God, she was such a *woman*. She was the one who was scaring him.

"Look at Phoebe," he said, and she turned toward the back window and laughed with him even though she couldn't really see anything. Her right eye had gone dark and her left was looking at the top of the seat. "I'm not hurtin' her, Phoeb. I swear."

The dog barked.

"Tell her," he whispered.

"I'm okay, Phoebe."

The dog jumped out of the box and up on the passenger's side door.

"Don't—"

Too late. Sally had already opened the door, and the dog was in her lap.

"Cut it out, Phoeb. I didn't break her. Down!"

Phoebe sat on the floor and laid her head on Sally's thigh.

Sally stroked her silky head. "The physician's assistant's assistant. We girls look after each other, don't we, Phoebe?"

"You can tell she's never been parking."

"It can be almost as much fun as skinny-dipping." Sally smiled into the big, round eyes looking up at her from her lap.

"And almost as risky," Hank said. But he still had his arm around her shoulders, and she loved the way it felt.

"I won't hurt him either, Phoebe. I swear."

* * *

Hoolie came out of the bunkhouse to meet them as soon as they parked his truck.

"You had a call from your favorite neighbor," he told Sally. "Claims a loose horse caused him to run into the ditch. I drove all the way up to his place and back, didn't see nothin'. No horse, no fence down, nothin'. Did you see anything?"

"We saw horses." Hank tossed Hoolie his keys. "Nice ride."

"They're right where they're supposed to be," Sally said.

"Except the high one Damn Tootin' rode in on. He said he reported *the incident* to the sheriff. You know what he's tryin' to do, don't you?"

"Drive me to commit murder?"

"Build some kind of a case. You know how he loves to sue people."

"Good. We'll kick his ass in court. That might be more fun than murder."

"Maybe he's trying to wear you down." Hoolie planted his hands on his indeterminate hips. "Keep you dancin' till you drop."

Sally sighed. "The trouble is he's got friends in high places."

"So do you," Hoolie said. "Maybe not so much around here, but there's high places all over the country, and they're full of horse lovers."

"Good point." Sally glanced at Hank. "The trouble is, sometimes those high places are too far off. All politics is local."

"A politician is your friend until he gets a better offer."

"*The trouble is* we don't have any more to offer."

"I didn't say *more*. I said better." Hoolie folded his arms. "Don't dance for him. You can put your energy to better use. Not to mention your considerable imagination."

"Another good point." She smiled. "Thank you for persisting in making it."

"No trouble." He stepped back. "I'll say good night, then."

Hank took his keys from his pocket, clicked the remote and whistled for Phoebe.

"Where are you going?" Instantly, Sally wished she could call back the question, or at least the anxious tone.

"Nowhere. Putting Phoebe to bed and getting my stuff."

"You're making her sleep in the pickup? Phoebe!" The dog perked her ears, but she stood her master's ground. "Oh, Hank, she can come in the house with you."

"You keep your dog in the house?" He sounded surprised. "We go by house rules."

"Baby has her own corner in the bunkhouse. We

have a cat in the house, but she doesn't believe in dogs. She barely acknowledges people. I'll bet Phoebe's used to sleeping with you."

"The Lakota don't sleep with their dogs," he said. "Phoebe sleeps wherever I put her bed. Where do you want her?"

"I didn't mean to insult you. I just didn't want you to think you had to—"

He challenged her with a hard look and a harder stance. "What's the big damn deal about my sleeping arrangements?"

"It's no big damn deal. You do what you want. I just want Phoebe to be comfortable."

"Comfortable? Okay, she likes to sleep on the east side of the house near an outside door and an open window on a feather bed."

"That can be arranged." She spun away and tripped.

He caught her. "What's wrong, Sally?"

"Defensive clumsiness. When I get rattled, I spaz out sometimes. Great way to ruin a dramatic gesture." She glowered. "What's your excuse?"

"Defensive gruffness."

"That's against house rules, but we'll call it even since it sounded like good ol'-fashioned sarcasm to me. I can hardly fault anybody for that." She signaled, "No penalty."

"You sure you want me to bring her bed in the house?"

"I'm sure this dog gets every vaccination and preventive treatment on any vet's list. So I want you to put her bed where the sun don't shine—" she smiled "—in the afternoon."

He hauled his duffel bag and Phoebe's denim pillow into the house and settled the dog down. He wasn't kidding about the outside door. Then he followed Sally through the living room, around the stairs, and down the hall, where they crossed paths with a calico cat, which scampered up the stairs.

"This is my room," Sally said of the first door in the hall. "It's also my office. Next is the main bath. I'll work around your shower schedule." She pushed the last door open and flipped the light on. "I'm putting you in this room because Zach and Annie have the upstairs. This used to be Grandma's room, which is why everything's purple. But now it's a guest room. I think you'll be comfortable. The trees shade the windows and keep it cool. There's a half bath through there. Say the word if you need anything. Help yourself in the kitchen anytime, anything you want. There's a TV in the den, just off the living room. And, um…" She looked up at him. "Thank you for doing this for us."

"No trouble."

"That I can't guarantee. Sleep well."

"You, too. I enjoyed the tour."

She gave a little nod, a wistful smile. She didn't

KATHLEEN EAGLE   83

quite know what to make of him, and he hadn't quite
decided what to do with her.

It was going to be an interesting three weeks.

Chapter Four

"Kevin's back," Hoolie announced as he came thumping in the back door. "Add one for supper. Any coffee left?"

"It's cold, but you can nuke it. I'm brewing iced tea."

Sally laid aside the ice pack she'd been using on her right eye and filled the teakettle. Hoolie was still banging around in the mudroom, and she was only getting about half of what he was saying, but she'd catch up on the rerun. He had a habit of repeating himself, especially if one of the teens court-ordered to work at the sanctuary was giving him trouble.

"So I've got him ridin' fence along the highway," was the upshot as he clomped into the kitchen. "You know damn well there was no horse on the road, but that don't mean Tutan didn't put another hole in the fence to back up his story. We got some volunteers set to help cut hay this weekend. So Hank and me, we're gonna…" He noticed the ice pack. "You feelin' okay, big sister?"

"I'm not okay with that question." Cold packs were her standard first-line remedy, and they were helping. Loss of vision in one eye wasn't unusual with multiple sclerosis, but neither was remission. She'd had this problem before and regained a good measure of sight back. She'd do it again without losing ground anywhere else. Not for a good long while.

She closed the microwave door on his cold coffee and pressed the button. "My health is my business. I want nothing but positive health vibes. That wheelchair is staying in the basement. There's only one person around here who needs a cane."

"Crutch."

"This reprieve could last for months. Years, maybe."

"Trouble with your eye again?"

"A little, but I'm loading up on vitamins." She believed in vitamins. Exercise, meditation, hydrotherapy—she believed in believing. She popped the microwave open and handed Hoolie his coffee. "You and Hank are going to what?"

"Move the cows."

"You can't ride with that ankle."

"I'm not okay with that order." He pulled two chairs away from the kitchen table, sat in one and propped his foot with its dirtier-by-the-day cast on the other. "I'm taking this damn thing off. My foot itches. That means the mummy boot has been on long enough."

"What does Hank say?"

Hoolie questioned her with a look.

"He's a professional."

"You ask him about your eye, and I'll ask him about my ankle."

"No deal." She snatched the whistling kettle off the stove. "I know more about MS than most doctors. These symptoms come and go. Eventually, some of them come and stay, but I'm not on any fast track to eventually." She pointed to his ankle. "*That* is going to heal. Give it time, and it'll go the way of all your other previously broken bones."

"My health is my business," he echoed in an irritating falsetto.

"Not when all your stories end with *I got the scars to prove it.*"

"I tell it like I remember it. The truth is always in there somewhere." He sipped his coffee. "I said I'd look after you."

"Look all you want. Just don't talk about it." She laid a hand on his bony shoulder. "I'll ride with Hank. We'll move the cows, and then we'll ride out to Coyote Creek and see if we can get a look at the Don."

"If something happens, you tell him why. You wouldn't fall so much if you'd keep a cane handy when you get tired or—"

"Three weeks." She squeezed his shoulder. "That's all I'm asking."

Hank was finishing up the hooves on the saddle horses when Sally came looking for him in the barn. From the first, he'd had her figured for a night person. Seemed he was right. Their ships would be passing mid to late morning, which was fine by him. Hoolie had filled him up with a hearty breakfast while they planned a few things out. He met one of the helpers he kept hearing about—Indian kid named Kevin Thunder Shield, who showed up ready to ride. Hoolie hooked the kid up with a horse and gave him an assignment, but Hank couldn't let the gelding go without a hoof trimming. And he wasn't herding any cattle until the rest of the saddle horses got the same treatment.

"That looks great," Sally said of the third set of hooves he'd filed. "You are *good.*"

"The trim's the important part. Right, girl?" He patted the black mare's rump. She'd behaved well. Hard to believe she'd ever been wild. "The shoes are icing on the cake. It's getting the right trim that makes the difference for most horses."

"We go easy on the icing around here."

"And that's fine. These horses don't have to hang out in stalls and watch their toenails grow. Except that one." He pointed to a big gray gelding. "Without shoeing that crack will keep growing."

Sally ran her hand down the horse's leg toward the hoof. "I didn't see that."

"I'll take care of it when we get back. Hoolie and me, we're gonna do some cowboyin'."

She straightened and faced him with folded arms. "You were going to let Hoolie ride with that cast on his foot?"

"I was gonna ride with Hoolie. Figured he could do what he wanted with his foot."

"Any objection to riding with me?"

He shrugged. "I'm here to help out."

"Weak," she warned.

"Let me try again. Objection? Hell, no. My pleasure."

"That's the spirit." She gave a tight smile. "I'm an excellent cowboy."

"I don't doubt it."

She sighed and put her arms around the big gray gelding's neck, nuzzling his thick black mane. "But I was hoping to ride Tank."

"Tank?" Hank chortled. "I'll have Tank retreaded for you by tomorrow." He started loading his files and nippers into his shoe box. "I thought I'd try a Double D mustang. Maybe Zach has some started. I'm a pretty good finisher."

"Me, too."

"Once they're green broke, I can put a nice handle on 'em."

"I'll bet." She raked her fingers through the gelding's mane. "Tank was my first adoption. When I picked him out ten years ago, he was as wild as they come. I was a stock contractor back then, but Tank really opened my eyes."

Hank eyed the horse. "He's no Spanish Mustang."

"Of course not. Like so many wild horses, he's got a lot of draft blood in him. You know, a lot of them just sort of walked off into the sunset back in the days when farmers started going horseless. And during the Depression, when they were going homeless. Tank's forebears were equine hobos." She unhooked one of the horse's crossties. "Can't you just see them running across a herd of mustangs in the Badlands? Freeee at last!" she whinnied, and Tank's ears snapped to attention.

Hank couldn't help smiling. "Until they got their farm-boy asses kicked."

"This big steel-drivin' man's gonna fix your hoof, Tank, so let's let that remark pass." She hooked a lead rope to the halter, scratched the horse's neck, and he lowered his head. "If he calls you farm boy, he's Henry," she said in the horse's ear.

"Nothin' wrong with Henry."

"I didn't say there was. Some of my best friends are named Henry."

"Hoolie?" he asked. She nodded. "Like I said, it's a good backup name. What's yours? Bet your mama didn't name you Sally."

"Ain't tellin'. It's a good name, but it doesn't fit me, so I don't use it." She pointed to a small buckskin gelding. "I'm riding him. He fits me well. We call him Little Henry."

Hank cracked up.

They rode side by side, soaking in sights and sounds and smells of summer in South Dakota without talking much. It was enough to point out the circling hawk, the coyote on the hill, the hidden gopher hole and to keep riding, keep looking and listening to the birds in the air, the insects in the grass, the thump-swish-thump of their mounts. It all felt right to Hank, as though he, too, had found a fit. Be damned if he'd try to work up some discomfort over feeling comfortable, not while it was working for him. This feeling was sacred.

He'd gotten away from the traditional practices his parents' generation had struggled to take back from obscurity—ceremonies nobody wanted to explain and a language hardly anybody used—but he'd soaked up the stories. The People had emerged from the Black Hills. *Paha Sapa.* White Buffalo Calf Woman had given them the pipe, and the horse—*Sunka Wakan,* or sacred dog—had given them a leg up in a land only the Lakota truly understood and appreciated in its natural state. It was grassland. Pull the grass up by the roots, and the earth would fly away. Tell the river how to run, and you would pay a price that had less to do with money than with home. And home, for the Lakota, had less to do with a place to live than with a place to walk.

Preferably a dry one.

Hank loved the stories and honored the wisdom even if he'd taken up a different kind of medicine. Even if he'd let his family fall apart—the traditional Lakota's worst nightmare—he believed that all people were relatives. All things? Being equal—not in this lifetime. But being relative? Sure. Relative to family life, being alone sucked.

Relative to reservation life, the old ways were healthy and holy. Relative to urban life, the reservation wasn't half bad.

But relative to anyplace he'd ever been—and he'd been all over—the vicinity of the Black Hills felt right.

The Double D was southeast of the Hills, but Hank could see their silhouette looming at the edge of the grasslands like a hazy purple mirage, a distant village of ghost tipis. The sight was beyond beautiful. Its power worked his soul's compass like polar magnetism. His whole body knew what it was about. It had been years since he'd pushed cattle on horseback, and while the method hadn't changed, he realized the madness was gone. He was no longer the angry young man who resented the cattlemen who leased the Indian land its owners couldn't afford to use. It didn't matter that none of the animals belonged to him or that the land they were crossing was claimed by someone else. He was one with the horse, and the woman who rode abreast of him functioned easily as his partner. Cows moved willingly as long as their calves bleated regularly to check in. They must have known the grass was greener wherever they were headed. Maybe they trusted Sally not to let them down. They belonged to her, after all. They must have known something.

You've never had much luck with women, Night Horse. Maybe you should take it from her animals. Just go along with her. Nothing to worry about.

Either that or just take it. Take as much as she offers. Hell, the first few weeks are always the best.

Hank drew in a whole chestful of clean Black Hills air. He had a bad habit of thinking too deep and breathing too shallow. He was attracted to this woman, pure and simple. Thinking only complicated the matter.

Stop thinking, Night Horse. Enjoy the pure and simple. She's pure. You're simple.

Sally loved the way her world looked from the top of a horse. The way Little Henry's gait made her hips move, the way he smelled, the way he snorted and strutted and swished his tail and made her sit up a little straighter, feel just slightly bigger than life—she loved every heady detail. But put the joy of sitting her horse together with the pleasure of watching Hank sit his, and Sally was all sweet spot. Watching him swing down from the saddle and open a wire gate gave her goose bumps. Pushing the cattle through the gate gave a taste of success, and making it happen together rubbed her utterly the right way.

She watched him muscle the wire loop over the top of the gate post, admired his easy mount, lit up inside when he looked her way as if to say, *What can I do for you now?*

"Follow me," she called out. "Let's take a ride to the wild side."

Little Henry pricked his ears, and Sally shifted her weight and gave him his head. She bid her hat good riddance as the wind rushed through her hair. Hank could have flown past her if he wanted to—his mare was faster than her little gelding—but he gave his horse cues according to her pace. When they reached the creek, Little Henry splashed right in. The crossing required a few yards of swimming this time of year, but nothing major.

For Sally.

She *whooped* and the water *swooshed* as Little Henry bounded up on dry land. Wet to the hip, she was loving every drop of water, every ray of sunshine, every bit of breeze. She circled her mount and saw Hank eyeing the water warily from the opposite bank.

"Don't worry," she called out. "She's a good swimmer."

"I'm not."

"You don't have to be. I promise."

He looked up at her. He'd held on to his hat, but clearly he wasn't so sure about the value of her promise.

"I can go back and lead you across."

"Hell, no." He continued to stare at the water. "What's my horse's name?"

"Ribsy."

"What kind of a name is that for a horse?"

"It's from a book. My sister named her." What difference did it make? What the heck was in a horse's name? He wasn't moving. Wasn't looking at anything but the water. Needed a moment, maybe. "My sister, the teacher. It's a kid's book." No connection. "Ribsy's Henry's best friend." Still no movement. "Ribsy's a dog."

He looked up. "This horse is named after a dog?"

"*Henry and Ribsy.* Ribsy's a dog."

"*Hoka Hey!*" Hank called out as he nudged the mare with his boot heels.

She took the plunge. Hank kept his seat, and the big black easily ferried him across the water. He looked a little sallow, but his dignity was still intact.

"What did you call me?" Sally asked, grinning like a proud instructor. "Hooker something?"

"I said, *Hoka Hey!* It's a good day to die." He leaned forward and patted the mare's neck. "*Sunka Wakan.*"

"That's right," she enthused. "It means *holy dog*, doesn't it? Well, there you go. Ribsy, Phoebe and me, we're your destiny. Stick with us, and your hydrophobia will be cured."

"What's that?" He glanced back at the murky water. "A monster with a bunch of arms?"

"I think that's a hydra."

"Yep. They're all down there." He looked up at her and smiled sheepishly as he joined her on the high ground. "Kind of embarrassing. I had a bad experience when I was a kid."

"Maybe you should try a different war cry."

They covered a lot of ground and saw a couple of eagles, a few deer and a few dozen mustangs before they found Don Quixote, a stout bay who'd surrounded himself with the prettiest mares on the Double D. There were roans and paints, mouse-brown grullos, buckskins and "blondies." After what had turned out to be a more tiring ride than she'd expected, Sally was energized simply by the sight of them, mainly courtesy of her left eye. But the vision of blue sky, green grass, striated hills and a motley band of mustangs was glorious. She didn't have to see Hank's excitement. She could feel it. His rapt interest was palpable.

"Let's get down for a while," he said quietly, as though speaking might disturb something.

She nodded. He must have sensed her weariness

because he swung to the ground and came to her, and she dismounted with far less grace than she would have wished. He noticed. He didn't say anything, but he took her full weight in his arms, drew her up to him and recharged her with a deep, delicious kiss.

It wasn't until he took his lips from hers that she realized she couldn't feel her right leg. She had to hang on to him—not that she didn't want to, but not for this reason.

"You made the earth move under my feet," she said. "Either Night Horse or Charley horse, I'm not sure—ah!" The sound of sharp pain was an innocent lie, if there was such a thing. Everybody understood pain, at least to some extent. Numbness was harder to explain.

"Damn cousin Charley's beatin' my time." He supported her against his right side. "Can't let him get away with it." He brought the horses along on the left and found a little grass for everybody on the shady side of a clump of chokecherry bushes.

"Better already." Her butt welcomed contact with good old terra firma, but she felt obliged to protest. "I'm okay now."

"Not so fast. I know how to—"

"Seriously, it's coming back."

"That's Charley for you. Right calf?" He massaged with practiced hands. She didn't feel much at first, but her nerves responded steadily to his gentle kneading. "This can be a sign of calcium deficiency."

"I'll load up on it tomorrow."

"I'm a big believer in truth and supplements for all."

"Good to know."

"Better?"

"Infinitely. Like your talents." Smiling, she grabbed his hand. "Wait. I think he's moving into my feet."

"Sorry, Charley," he quipped as he slid his hands down to her boot.

She stilled them with hers. "I'll take a rain check."

"Sounds good." He went to his saddle and brought back the canvas pack he'd tied behind the cantle. Squatting on his heels, he took out a bottle of water and cracked open the plastic cap. "It might be warm, but it's wet."

"You think of everything." She took a long drink.

"Second nature when you spend your life on the road."

"I'll bet you're starving. I do have supper waiting in the refrigerator. I almost brought something along, but then I thought, no, we'll be sweaty and dirty, and we'll appreciate it more after we get back, and it's nice and fresh and…" She handed him the bottle. "Annie would have packed a nice picnic. She's like you. She thinks of everything."

He took a drink from the bottle and laughed. "It's just water."

"I'm easy." She smiled. "Simple pleasures. I don't do this often enough. I used to ride out here all the time, but it's become…" She gazed at the bluffs in the distance. "I've become lazy. It's easier to hop in the pickup. And now that Zach's come on board…"

"You don't get out here in a pickup. It's too rough."

"And we don't want this area disturbed by anything motorized." She pointed west. "There's some public land beyond those hills. Very isolated. And there's tribal land adjoining that." She swung her hand in a northerly arc. "If…*when* we get those new leases, we'll almost double our carrying capacity. The Tribal Council has been very supportive of our program, but Dan Tutan's been leasing it forever, and he pays practically nothing for grazing permits on the public land. He has his own support from Pierre all the way to Washington."

"You're running publicly protected wild horses for the Bureau of Land Management, aren't you? You should get preference. Plus, if you've got the Tribal Council…"

"We have the majority. We're…pretty sure we do."

"You can never be too sure about those Indians."

"I'm not too sure about *you*." She smiled. "But I know what *assume* makes out of me." She lifted one shoulder. "And Tutan's been taking us all for granted for far too long. He knows how to work the system. Like anything involving property, it's all about location."

"Tell us about it." He glanced at the barren draw below. "I've got some beachfront reservation land for sale. Complete with a big bridge."

"I'll take it," she enthused. "Where do I sign?"

"I'll have my people draw up the treaty." He adjusted his hat by the brim, leaned back on his elbows and eyed her for a moment. "You've got a good thing goin' here. Why push it?"

"Because we can." She leaned closer. "Because the push needs to be made. More needs to be done, and we can do it. All we have to do is show that our program is viable, that we can handle more land, more stock, and we're in the catbird's seat. Tutan's free rein over the range will soon be over. For a considerable piece of these grasslands, it's back to nature."

"This part doesn't look like it's ever been away."

"My father never got much use out of this part of the ranch. He would have sold it, but back then there weren't any takers. But the takers are…" The look in his eyes set her back on her heels. *The takers are what? The takers are who?* "I don't want to take any more land. I want to set some aside, and I'm willing to pay for the privilege of standing aside." She smiled. "Pay with what? you may ask. My sister asks every other day. I have to get creative about getting more public support."

"I seem to recall some mention of a plan."

"Plan? What plan?" Mock innocence was one of her favorite shticks.

"It was on hold for the wedding. Then you had to get the honeymoon back on track. You are one smooth operator, Sally." He plucked a droopy-headed grass stem and stuck it in the corner of his mouth. "So, what's the plan, and how many days before you have it in place? You've got what? Twenty-one?"

"Give or take." She smiled. "Sam told the newly-weds to stay as long as they wanted."

"And Zach told me if I had any problems, he could be back in twenty-four hours."

"No worries, mate."

"If I were a worrier, the words *creative* and *plan* might give me pause."

"I'm glad you're not." Arms around her legs, she drew her knees up for a chin rest. "Because if I had a plan, I'd really want to tell you about it. I would *really* value your thoughts. You strike me as a practical man. And I'm a creative woman." She gave a slow, sensual smile. "Yin and yang."

"Hmm. If I were a thinking man, my first thought would be…" He winked. "Somebody's yin-yangin' my chain."

She groaned. "Is that what passes for humor where you come from?"

"Well, there's Indian humor, and there's edumacated Indian humor."

"Edumacated?"

"Half-assed educated, which is a dangerous thing."

"Zach says you're the best doc he knows."

"If they ain't broke, I can fix 'em up good enough for the next round. You can't take the cowboy out of the rodeo unless he's out cold. Then he can't argue." He tossed his chewed grass. "'Course, I'm not a doctor. Started out to be, got myself edumacated."

"Meaning?"

"Got married, had a kid, dropped out of school."

"Happens to a lot of us. Even without the marriage and kid part." She thought twice, but it wasn't enough to stop her. "What happened to your son?"

"He got hit by a car. He was in a coma for six months. By the time he died…" He drew a long, deep breath and sighed. "By the time we let him go, we had nothin' left." He lifted one shoulder as he scanned the hills. "Bottom line, I thought she was watchin' him, she thought I was watchin' him." He shook his head, gave a mirthless chuckle. "It's not the bottom line that kills you. It's all the garbage you have to wade through before you find it. And when you do, hell, there's no way to forgive if you can't even look at each other anymore."

Sally could not speak. Her throat burned, and she knew it would be a mistake to open her mouth. She knew hospitals. Technicians with their tests, nurses with their needles, doctors with no answers—she knew them all. She imagined them easily. She knew what it felt like to be poked and prodded and eye-balled. It could be painful. It was often scary. When it became part of life's routine, it was miserable, maddening, frustrating, and it hurt. Physically, when it was your own body, it hurt. Sometimes you thought, *if this kills me, that'll be it. Over and out.* She could imagine that part. Easily. What she could not imagine was sitting beside the bed rather than lying in it, watching over your child, losing your child piece by piece until finally the terrible word had to be said.

She reached for his hand. He flinched, but she caught him before he could draw away and kissed him, there on the backs of his healing fingers, rough knuckles, tough skin. She met his wary gaze. Her eyesight was a little hazy, but her heart was not. Whatever she was feeling, it wasn't pity. Wouldn't give it, couldn't take it.

He smiled, just enough to let her know he understood.

"So." He glanced away, withdrew his hand, gave a brief nod. "Back to the plan."

Hank thought it over on the ride back. She was pretty quiet—must've talked herself out—and he had time to watch the evening sky begin to change colors while he thought about the land, the horses, Sally and her big plan. She wanted to publicize the merits of the sanctuary and the appeal of owning a once-wild horse. She'd done some Internet research and pitched the idea of a documentary, but only a couple of documentary producers had responded, and they'd said the story had been done. She needed a new angle.

"I have a killer idea that I haven't told anybody about except Hoolie. And now you." Her secret Henrys, she'd called them, but he couldn't see her keeping any secrets the way this one had tumbled out of her. She wanted to hold a competition for horse trainers. They would choose a horse from the best of the three- and four-year-olds, and they would commit to conditioning, gentling and training the horse to perform. She would bring in experienced judges, award *big, huge* cash prizes and auction off the horses. "It's got everything," she'd claimed. "History, romance, suspense, sports, gorgeous animals in trouble, beautiful people who care, and lots and lots of money."

Hank had enjoyed the sound of her enthusiasm so much, he hadn't asked whether the beautiful people cared about the animals or the money. He hadn't asked where the money would come from. Maybe Zach's brother, Sam, would sponsor the whole thing. He'd hit the jackpot, and he seemed like a good guy.

Covering the last mile between a job well done and supper, Hank knew one thing about the woman riding at his side: she lived for wild horses. She was the real Mustang Sally. She was serious about her dream, and no matter how big the undertaking, she would do what she had to do to make it come true. He was sure she had him figured into her doings somehow. It would be fascinating to watch the woman roll out the rest of her strategy. She'd already shown him she could get something out of him he never, *ever* gave.

Now it was his turn. She was keeping something close to the chest, some heavy weight that bore down on her. He'd seen it knock her over. He'd watched her get right back up. He wouldn't press her—she had enough pressure—but she was going to have to strip off more than her clothes. Whatever she was figuring him for, trust would be the price for Night Horse insurance.

They crossed paths with Hoolie on his way out the back door. The way he said *hope you two had a nice time* made it sound like he was mad about something— supper, maybe, although he said he and Kevin hadn't waited—and Hank questioned Sally with a look. She smiled, shrugged it off, said *we did* to the slamming door. "Grumpy old men," she stage-whispered.

"I got twenty-twenty hearing, big sister."

"I love you, too, ya big grump." She lowered her voice. "The older he gets, the more he sounds like a mother hen."

"Thirty-thirty," was the rejoinder from the yard.

"Shoot me, then," Sally called back, eyes sparkling. "Chicken sandwich anyone?" she whispered.

She wasn't kidding about the chicken. Hank was used to cold suppers, but not like this. Sally piled on the fruits and vegetables, fresh-picked garden greens, potato salad and whole-grain bread. At first glance, it struck him as a woman's kind of meal. At first bite, a man found himself taking his time. No rush to fill up when there was taste and talk on the table.

"I think your plan for a horse-training contest could work." He could tell he had her at *work,* but he added, "I'd compete."

"I was hoping you'd help me run it."

"That wouldn't play to my strong suit. I'm not much of a runner." He leaned back in his chair and eyed her thoughtfully. "Especially behind a friend's back. What do the newlyweds think about running a contest?"

"They're on their honeymoon, for which I thank you very much." Sally popped a green grape into her mouth. "Annie thinks we've already bitten off more than we can chew. She's very careful, very conservative."

"And she married a cowboy?"

"You toss *careful* and *conservative* out the door when you fall in love. At least, that's what I've heard." She went for another grape. "I don't have time for *conservative.* Or patience. I know it's a virtue, but time doesn't stand still while we take small bites and chew thoroughly. This land and these horses look tough, but they're vulnerable. They're right for each other— they *need* each other. We've come a long way getting them back together, and we can't backtrack. Every acre we add to our program is home for another horse." She lifted one shoulder. "Okay, a tenth of a horse, which is why we need more acres. They need space. Wide-open space. You can't have wild horses without wild places."

"I'm down with you on wildness, but I'm no organizer."

"I just need an able-bodied ally. Somebody who knows horses." She leaned toward him. "You wouldn't have to stick around. Just help me get started. Back me up."

"I'm not from this reservation," he reminded her. "I can back you up, but you're always gonna have holdouts on the council."

"I know, but you're cousins, right?"

"We're all related."

"I'm not saying you all look alike to me. The Oglala and the Hunkpapa are like cousins, aren't they? And you're Hunkpapa."

"A woman who knows her Indians." He gave half a smile.

"Not *my* Indians. And I know cousins compete with each other, just like sisters do."

"When we say *all my relatives,* we mean you, too."

"But you don't include *Damn Tootin'*. He's all about Tutan, and nobody else."

"We won't let him in the circle or the contest," Hank assured her. "I'm here for you, Sally. For three weeks. What do you want me to do?"

"I've already written a proposal, and the BLM is

sending someone out to look me over. Basically make sure I can do what I said I could do, which is set the thing up and make it happen."

"And your sister doesn't know about any of this?"

"I want to see if it's even feasible first. I need to pass muster with the bureaucrats so they'll let us use the horses this way. If the BLM approves, I know Annie and Zach will be thrilled. And won't that be some wedding present?" She reached across the table and laid her hand on his arm. "Just help me look good, okay? Me and the horses."

"You look fine, Sally. You and the horses."

"Thanks." She drew a deep breath. "My only other worry is Tutan and his little shenanigans. Not to mention his connections."

"You know…" He turned his arm beneath her hand and drew it back until their palms slid together. "I don't like Tutan."

"He doesn't know his Indians." She smiled and pressed her hand around his. "Why didn't you tell him the Night Horse who worked for him was your father?"

"I'm not tellin' him anything." He lifted one shoulder. "He's probably checked me out, probably knows by now."

"What happened?" she asked gently.

"My father had some problems, but he wasn't afraid to work." He looked into her eyes, saw no prejudgment, no preemptive pity. Nothing but willingness to listen. "Jobs are hard to find on the reservation, so he'd go wherever the work was and do whatever he was asked to do. He used to hire on for Tutan, and he'd be gone for weeks at a time.

"Come deer season, Tutan liked to have weekend hunting parties for his friends—probably some of those important connections you're talking about—and he'd take one of his hired hands along to bird-dog for him. You know, beat the brush, flush out the game. Half those guys didn't know the butt from the barrel, but they knew how to party."

"Which resulted in the so-called hunting accident."

"Out there alone, got drunk, fell on his gun." He shook his head. "Tragic."

"How old were you?"

"Old enough to know that dog wouldn't hunt. Not unless he was on somebody's payroll." He shook his head. "He wouldn't take my brother and me hunting. Said he'd had enough of it when he was a kid. He didn't hunt for sport. He called and said he wasn't coming home that weekend because Mr. Tutan's friends wanted to do some hunting, and Dad was gonna make some extra cash.

"He'd been dead for weeks when they found him. Tutan had about as much to say as he did the other night. He thought John Night Horse had gone home after he'd drawn his last wages for the season. Tutan didn't post his land, so, sure, hunters came around all the time, but nobody had stopped in that weekend, friends or otherwise."

"So it could have been an accident."

"I didn't think so, but who listens to a twelve-year-old kid?"

"What about your mother?"

"People believe what they want to believe, she said. Indian blood is cheap. Accidents, suicide, murder—what's the difference? Dead is dead. And she proved that by dying when I was fifteen."

"What do you believe?" she asked softly.

"I believe life is life." He gave her hand a gentle squeeze. "From first breath to last, it's up to you to live it in a good way."

"I'll drink to that." She took up her water with her free hand, paused mid-toast and took a closer look at her glass. "What about blood? Are some kinds dearer than others?"

"You're lookin' at one Indian whose blood ain't cheap." He waited for her eyes to actually meet his. "O positive. Universal donor." He smiled. "Priceless."

Chapter Five

Sally was up early.

She'd checked her e-mail—the honeymooners had landed safely and a group of church campers wanted to schedule a day trip to the sanctuary—and paid some bills online before leaving the room that had served variously as the "front" bedroom, the den, the office and now all three rolled up into Sally's lair. She refused to consider it her confines, but there were times when parts of her body wouldn't do much. For Annie's sake she came out for meals, but otherwise she worked long hours in the office. She profiled every animal on the place, recorded every piece of machinery, kept the books, researched everything from parasites to nonprofits and hatched plans. Her motto was: When the Moving Gets Tough, the Tough Get Moving. One of these days she was going to stitch up the words into a little plaque.

Just as soon as she learned to stitch, which wasn't happening anytime soon. Not as long as the good times were walkin' instead of rollin'.

She helped herself to coffee, popped an English muffin in the toaster and glanced out the back window.

Here came Grumpy.

She couldn't get it through Hoolie's head that as long as she could get up and go, she was going. He knew as well as she did that her physical condition was predictably unpredictable. Most people didn't believe they could get seriously sick or hurt anytime. They *knew* it, but they didn't *believe* it. Sally remembered what that carefree, wasted-on-the-healthy frame of mind was like. She'd been there, BMS—before multiple sclerosis. MS had made a believer of her. Her body could turn on her anytime. Just a matter of time.

She'd had to admit that her eye had been bothering her. She was in the knowing-but-not-really-believing stage—was that the same as denial?—but Hoolie couldn't be denied. He was old and dear, and he knew better. Annie was young and dear, and she could be put off. So, yes, she'd been waking up some mornings—just *some*—feeling like she had something in her right eye. And sometimes—like the other night in the pickup with Hank—it would totally blur up as though she were crying Vaseline. Weird. These things often hit her when she was feeling stressed, which was hardly what she'd been feeling that night.

Hoolie mounted the back steps, crutch thumping, black shepherd in tow. He told the dog to stay outside, but she took off as soon as the door closed, presumably in search of somebody else to herd.

"Have you guys *edumacated* Phoebe and Baby yet?" The word was Hank's. She felt giddy about knowing it and saying it, like a girl with a crush. She laughed at the funny look Hoolie gave her. "Hank's teaching me to talk Indian. He got himself *edumacated.* I guess it's learning the hard way."

"Seems like a real smart fella. Zach says he's halfway to bein' a doctor and twice as good as most of them he knows. Guess he's met a few." He glanced down at his cast. "So, if I have any more trouble with this, I can probably…you know…"

"Ask him to take a look. I doubt if he'd charge you much." She pulled a chair out from the table and spun it around. "You know, you're supposed to use two crutches."

He ignored the comment, but he accepted the chair.

"I didn't mean to get testy last night. You were gone a long time, and it's been a while since you've been on a horse."

"It was wonderful." She positioned a second chair

for his footstool. "It was just what the halfway doctor would have ordered. *If* orders were in order."

"What's he chargin' for fixing up Tank's hooves? He's out there now gettin' set to work on him. You might wanna go watch and learn."

"Like I've never seen horseshoeing done before." She headed for the coffeepot.

"Not like this. Hank's firing up for a hot shoeing. Got his portable forge out. Took his shirt off. Got a nice set of tools all laid out." He nodded his thanks for the coffee she handed him. "Sometimes they charge extra for hot shoeing, but they say it's worth it."

She laughed. "If I didn't know you better, I'd say you were playing a game that has everything to do with firing up, nothing to do with horseshoes."

"Game? What game? I'm just sayin'…"

"I have a couple of volunteers coming in today, and I thought we'd get them started on—"

"Mowing the ditches along the right-of-way and putting up the new snow fence. I'm already on it." He raised one unruly eyebrow. "In case you wanted to take Hank something cold and wet, there's pop in the fridge."

"I don't want to give him the wrong idea. I'll just take him some ice water." *In a tall, sweaty glass.*

The smell of burning charcoal drifted through the barn's side door, where Sally was greeted by wagging tails and canine smiles. Phoebe and Baby were buds. The Dog Whisperer had spoken.

Her ear followed the soft metallic *tap tap tap* to the bright side of the barn where the big door stood open, the big gray gelding was cross-tied and the big bronze man wielded hammer over nail. Wearing a short leather apron over his jeans, Hank bent to the task supporting the horse's front leg on his knee, lining hoof up with shoe and chewing on a nail. His shoulders glistened, forearms flexed, hair curtained his face, sweat rolled down the side of his face. He looked magnificent.

He plucked the horseshoe nail from his mouth, lined it up, and spoke without sparing her a glance. "I had to score and burn the hoof a little bit above the crack. That's the key to keeping a quarter crack like this from reaching the corona. You keep shoes on him until the hoof grows out, he'll be fine. You say he's never been shod?" *Tap tap tap.*

"I didn't see that crack. I should've noticed."

"I'm not faulting you." He lowered the gelding's leg and straightened slowly. Maybe his back was stiff. More likely, he wanted to prolong the unfolding of his smooth, strapping, sweaty, dirt-streaked torso. He smiled. "I'm impressed with how cooperative he is."

"He's a good boy." She watched Hank out of the corner of her good eye as she patted the horse's flank. "Aren't you, Tanksy? You're still my boy. Henry isn't half as smooth as you are, so don't worry about being replaced."

"You have no idea." His hammer clanked into the wooden toolbox.

"I was talking about *Little* Henry. You thought I meant you? You've asked me not to call you that, so don't worry."

"Are you worried, Tank?" He scratched the horse's face. "Me, neither."

"I do love a smooth ride."

He nodded at her glass of water. "Is that for me?"

"You're welcome to it."

"Did you bring it for me?"

"Hoolie said you were out here in the hot, um…" She laughed and handed it to him. "I did. Hoolie suggested pop, but I thought water would be—"

"Thanks." In three long gulps he drained half the big tumbler.

Then he tipped his head back and let the water overflow the corners of his mouth, slide down his neck and over the hills and valleys of his chest. She watched his Adam's apple bobble once before he lifted the glass from his lips and dribbled the rest of the water over his face. A thin rivulet coursed quickly down the middle of his sleek torso and disappeared behind his belt buckle. She imagined it puddling in his belly button. Thank God she had perfectly clear vision in one eye.

Her gaze retraced its route slowly. She knew what she'd find when her train of thought reached the station. Dark-eyed male satisfaction. They loved it when a woman took the time to look, didn't mind letting it show that she liked what she saw.

"I could get you some more."

He gave a slow smile as he handed her the glass. "That hit the spot."

Touched off by his smile, her popgun laugh tickled her throat on its way out. Oh, she did like the way this man made her feel. She turned carefully—this was no time for an uneven keel—and froze halfway through her next step. And it was all his doing. His hand on her arm.

Instantly carefree, she reversed her turn and lifted her face for the kiss she felt coming. She hooked her arm over his shoulder and pressed the cool glass against his back. She felt the shock of it—or of her—shimmy through him, felt his damp heat against her breasts, smelled the fire from his portable forge and horse sweat and barn dust and the heady scent of Hank at work. She pressed close and kissed back and gave a sound of raw need and deep delight.

"Pardon my sweat," he whispered.

"It hit the spot." She giggled. A mortifying sound, but there it was, like a bee in a jar—a bright, girlish buzz in her throat. "Different strokes for different spots."

"Mmm." He let go of her arm as he stepped back, glancing at the smudge he'd left. "I stroked you a new one."

"Put your mark on me, did you?" She checked her arm, nodded, felt deliciously, dementedly silly. "I didn't mean to interrupt."

"Yeah, you did."

"I did. My boy needed a break." She glanced at the horse. "Tanks!" The animal raised his head. "You're quite welcome."

Hank chuckled. "I love me some comic relief. Have a seat, Sally. The show gets better."

"I believe it. I don't think I've ever been kissed by a man wearing an apron." Or one who hauled an anvil around. She took in the array of long handles extending from his toolbox—tongs and nippers, hammers and rasps. A bucket of water stood near the small, conical forge. "Why are you hot shoeing him? Because of the crack?"

"I pulled a side clip out of the shoe for support behind the crack. You want the hoof to grow out right, you make the right shoe." He lifted another steel masterpiece at the end of his tongs for closer inspection. "And if the shoe fits…"

"Mustangs rarely have hoof problems."

"Not if they have room to run on ground that isn't plowed or paved over."

"Or chopped up into small pastures and overgrazed." Disagreement over Western land management had raged around her all her life, but she'd taken up the opposite side of the land-use argument since her days as a rodeo stock contractor. Wildlife, including horses, needed protection. "I don't know what my father would think of what we've done with his ranch. He was a cattleman."

"You don't worry about what your neighbor says, do you?"

"Tutan? No. I worry about what he does, or what he could do. He acts like we're the ones who don't belong here, like the horses are intruding on his God-given grazing rights. Where does he get off, thinking he's entitled to use a piece of land any way he wants just because it's there?"

"Where I come from, we ask that question a lot." He poked through the nails in the tray on top of the toolbox.

She grimaced. "Serious case of the pot calling the kettle black, huh?"

"Maybe." He came up smiling. "After that kiss, I gotta wonder what else you've got cookin'."

She laughed. "I'm an acquired taste. At least that's what I'm told."

"Sounds complicated."

"And you're a meat-and-potatoes man?"

"Some people like to cover it all up with sauce, but I prefer to know what's in the pot." He ducked under the cross-tie and took up the next hoof on the far side of the horse. "Tell you what, Tank, if the kiss was any indication, she's not as complicated as she thinks she is."

She took the hint and walked away laughing.

* * *

Right.

And Hank wasn't champing at the bit to haul her back in his arms and ram his tongue down her throat.

Sally was a woman, the creature conceived for the sole purpose of complicating a man's life. She was what she thought she was and then some. Her kiss was complex, compounding his interest, confounding his brain. What did she want from him? Besides sex. That he could do, *would* do in his own good time and to their mutual satisfaction. She'd piqued his interest in more ways than one. But beyond a man's two or three straight-forward ways lay the mystifying maze of women's ways, where men could sure lose their way in a hurry.

Hank didn't care about the color of a pot so much as what it was made of and whether he could grab it by the handle without getting burned. Pretty damn hard to earn a living with blistered hands. He couldn't help wondering about that little hitch in her step as he watched her walk away.

Sashay away. Was that it? She was either flirting or hurting.

Or both. He couldn't help wondering.

He finished shoeing Tank, and then he trimmed Ribsy's hooves. He liked this work. He'd picked it up after Deborah left him. It was either fill his hands with tools or a bottle. He wouldn't want to do it full time— horseshoeing could be hard on the back—but what had started out as a therapeutic hobby had become a rewarding sideline, and working with his hands gave him time to clear his head.

Sally's interruption was like a paddle plunked in a pool. She'd stirred him up a little, but everything had cleared up when she went away.

Only she hadn't gone far. After he turned the horses out, he ran into her a few yards from the kitchen door. She was playing in real water, aiming a garden hose at a tiered planter with one hand, waving him down with the other.

"Come see the house that Zach built!"

"What house?" It looked like a huge green wedding cake with three metal scarecrows stuck into it.

"This strawberry planter. Sort of like a house."

Damn, that water looked good.

"The boys made this for us. They made these wonderful sculptures for us for Christmas. See, that's Zach with a bull." She pointed to a metal figure with a twist of sheet metal for a hat and contorted hay-rake tines serving as bowed legs and handlebar horns. "And Hoolie. And Kevin."

He studied the pieces of implement parts and scrap metal welded together, recognizing a head here, a couple of arms there, maybe a dog or a horse, another...

"And Hank!"

She blasted his ass with the hose.

If she was hoping for noise, she wasn't getting any. He turned and walked into the onslaught without hesitation, letting the water cool his chest, drench the front of his jeans, turn the dust on his boots to mud. It felt fine. Even better when he tossed his hat toward the house, took the hose from her hand, leaned over and turned the water on the back of his head. He raked it through his hair and then slurped a drink while he zeroed in on his next move. With his free hand he spun her around and shoved the end of the hose into the back of her pants.

"Eeeyiiiii!"

She snatched at the hose, grabbed, yanked and failed. "I'm caught!"

"Just barely dropped my line." He reached for the hose. "Here, stand—"

But she went down as though he'd pulled a rug out from under her, landed flat on her face in the mud.

"You okay? What happened?"

"Nothing! I tripped."

"I'm sorry. Here, let me—" her arm was tucked behind her back like a chicken wing, grappling with the hose, which she was about to dislodge "—turn it off."

"No! Leave it on. Leave it!"

"You'll slip." He stopped in his tracks. She wanted to play? He jumped over the spray she shot at him, wrested the hose away and offered her a hand. "I'm not goin' down with you if that's what you're thinkin'."

"I can do it." She waved his hand off. "I'm fine. I

can do it myself." Like a child with something to prove, she scrabbled to her feet. "See? Now…" She spread her arms wide. "Fire away. C'mon! With the hose."

"I just knocked you over with the hose."

"Bet you can't do it again." Hands on her hips, she stood firm. "Come on, hose me off."

A quick, cold shot bought Hank another round of music to his inner boy's ear. Her shrieks dissolved into laughter, at once sucking him in and drawing him out. She looked and sounded as fine as she claimed to be, and he had to laugh with her. She would have it no other way. The dogs got in on the act, and all four of them were soaked by the time Hank assumed the role of killjoy and turned off the water.

"Ah, that felt good," he admitted as they planted wet bottoms on the sun-warmed cement steps. "Now what? We go in and track up the floor, or we sit out here looking like two dogs left in the rain?"

"Speak for yourself." Sally puffed out her chest. Her wet white shirt had become a translucent third skin, her bra a silky second, and a hint of nipples the ultimate attraction. "I look like a cool cat."

"Am I your mirror?" He mussed her hair, and she countered with claw and yowl. "You do look cute."

She returned the hair mussing. "You do, too."

He nodded. "When are you gonna tell me what's goin' on with you?"

Her smile faded, and the light in her eyes dimmed.

He felt as though he'd hit her. It wasn't like him to pry, but he'd seen too many missteps, and he had a gut feeling.

He glanced away. He wouldn't ask again.

"Zach made that, huh?" He braced his elbows on his knees, laced his fingers together and stared at the planter. "When do I get some strawberries?"

"You like strawberries?" To his relief, she had perked up. "Would you rather have them for dessert tonight or breakfast tomorrow?"

"I'll take them whenever they're ready. I don't think I've ever had homegrown strawberries."

"How about homemade ice cream?" She smiled. "I've got you now, haven't I? My sister's the cook in the family, but we've got this great little machine that makes the best ice cream. That's my summertime specialty. Do you like watermelon?"

He grimaced.

"How about sweet corn? We planted tons of it. Annie's the gardener around here, too, but I really took an interest this year. The weather's been great. It feels good to dig around in the dirt. Good therapy."

"For what?"

"Anything. You name it, Doc."

"You're an interesting case. Mind if I look for a few more clues?"

"Knock yourself out."

"I've tried that, and think I'll pass." He gave a humorless chuckle. "Actually, I've done that, too. Down and out. From what I was told, it ain't pretty."

"When you're as clumsy as I am, you learn how to catch yourself."

"That's not what I see. You've learned how to *protect* yourself."

"Same thing."

"Uh-uh. I'm not a doctor, Sally, but I've done some doctoring."

"And I've done some knocking my head against the wall. Nothing a little session with Mother Earth can't cure. Down and dirty." She gave him her saucy Sally look, the one that made him itch in places it wasn't polite to scratch. "Down *in,* not out. Down deep and inside and underneath." She laid her hand on his thigh. "And you, my flawlessly fit friend with the healing hands, even you've stumbled."

"A time or two, yeah."

"And what did you do? You picked yourself up, hosed yourself off, got back in the game. Right? The more time you spend thinking about it, talking about it, picking it apart, the harder it is to get back up and get moving again." She gave him a merciless little pat before she took her hand away. "A time or two? Is that all? You're quite a paragon, Mr. Night Horse."

"Yep."

"You dry?"

"I've been dry for a while." Seven years. Lucky

seven. "I'll flip you for the shower." He pulled a quarter from his jeans. "What do you want?"

"Heads we go separate, tails we go in together."

Damn. "What do you want?"

"Ask me no questions, I'll tell you no lies." She had a half-scared look in her eyes that didn't match up with her smart mouth. "Figure it out."

She was pushing too hard, questioning herself, lying to herself, and he wasn't going there with her. He grabbed her shoulders and held her at forearm's length, willing her to give it up. Not her body. Her act. *Cut the crap, Sally.*

The look in her eyes was killing him. He covered her mouth with his and gave the kiss she had coming, the one that said *This is me, baby. Give me the real you.*

Her eyes were closed when he lifted his head. She opened them slowly, and for an instant she was his. But she promptly covered.

"That's a start," she tossed out, smiling too quickly. "There's nothing wrong with me that a little physical therapy can't put right."

"You're the damnedest woman I've ever met."

"That's what they all say."

"That won't work, either." He drew himself away. "I know people, Sally. I know when someone's been around the block a few times, and you haven't. We both have hurts, and yours didn't come from knocking yourself out. They're not of your own making." He flipped, slapped the coin on the back of his hand, and challenged her. "You either come clean with me or we ain't comin', Sally. At least not together. Heads or tails?"

"Be my guest."

Sally escaped directly to the laundry room. Three weeks. Was it too much to ask? Three weeks of remission, three weeks with a man, *this* man, *the same damn three weeks*. Couldn't she have her wish, her way for three, just *three* short weeks? She pulled a load of fluffy towels from the dryer, satisfied her nose with the fresh scent, and folded each one carefully, telling herself to straighten up, put her house in order, stop acting like a female in heat. He was willing to kiss her. He was a good kisser. It was something. She needed *something*.

Her armload of towels was something he needed, and when she heard the water running she told herself she would just slip them inside the bathroom door if the one from her room was open. The towel stand was within no-peek reach. The tub-shower combination was on the adjoining wall. The door hinges were quiet. There would be no disturbance.

As long as the curtain was closed, which it wasn't. As long as she didn't look in the mirror on the opposite wall, which she did. She would have backed away if she could have. She would have been able to if his astonishing body had presented itself to her right eye instead of her left, her good eye. But the stars were aligned for full disclosure, and her good eye was thrilled. His head was tipped back, his eyes closed, his chest taking on water, one hand braced on the wall and the other pleasuring himself.

Damn him. Why wasn't he letting her do that?

Any man who preferred his hand to a woman's body was just plain...

...not interested in the woman. For whatever reason.

Maybe it was just him.

More likely it was her. Her imperfect body.

Hell, nobody was perfect. Surely he knew that. *No body was perfect.*

Except maybe his. Damn, he looked delicious, all warm and wet and hard as rock candy. Her heart pounded, her mouth watered, and her throat went dry.

Was this what he called *coming clean?*

She called it a terrible thing to waste. She called it the worst travesty of justice she'd yet to confront, and she'd confronted some doozies. What god had she offended? Which goddess had abandoned her?

What in hell was she doing wrong?

Well, for one thing, she was staring. She unloaded the towels, stepped back, pulled the door almost shut, and then she committed the losing error. She lifted her gaze from his hand to his eyes. They were open, of course, and they had her dead to rights.

* * *

He came into the kitchen carrying his duffel bag.

She was sitting on a tall kitchen stool concentrating on keeping her hands from shaking while she shelled peas into a glass bowl. "Are you leaving?" she asked softly.

"No. I gave my word. I'll be back after I find a place to stay."

"Hank, I'm…" She sighed. She couldn't say it. She was feeling a riot of emotion, but sorry simply wasn't part of it. "You're the damnedest man I've ever met."

"Then I'd say you've met a lot of boys who only looked like men."

"You had your free look. Now I've had mine."

"Fair enough." He took a step closer, offering her no quarter. "The next one's gonna cost us both. We drop the play-acting and get real. No protection except a scrap of rubber."

"Get real? Haven't you had enough reality?"

"I don't know if I've had any."

"But that's what you're looking for?"

"If I'm looking for something, that would be it. I like your ass, Sally. Hell, I like your sass. What I don't like is the chip on your shoulder. I could knock it off, easy." He shook his head, lowered his voice. "But that wouldn't get us anywhere, would it?"

"Stay here, Hank." She pushed the bowl aside. "I really want you to stay here."

"What for?"

"For the sake of…" She lowered one leg, and her bare foot touched the floor, a cold shock. "For my sake. This chip is getting pretty heavy."

"Like I said…"

"I know, but it draws your attention, doesn't it?"

"A chip is a chip, honey. I've seen a lot of them. I know what they're about." The look in his eyes went from cold to kind. "Fear and pain."

"I'm not—"

"*I'm* not. I'm not your antidote." He waved his free hand as though sweeping cobwebs. "Let's clear the air, Sally."

She bristled. "Why? I like it steamy."

"I don't like feeling crowded. One minute we're getting to know each other, having a little fun, the next you're…" He scowled. "What do you want from me?"

"How does friendship with benefits strike you?"

"Like something out of a TV show." He gave half a smile, but the light went out of his eyes. "I can fly you to paradise on my benefits, but not for free. I'll babysit for free. You want peep shows? You want slap and tickle? That's extra."

"Wow." She clapped her hands. "Congratulations, cowboy. Way to slap my chip into next week."

"That's all it takes? You disappoint me."

"Sorry, but it's just not fair to talk about paradise

when you're throwing me under the straight-talk express."

He glowered at her. She glared right back.

One corner of his mouth twitched.

She smiled, straight up.

"Okay." He wagged his head, gave a reluctant chuckle. "Look, Sally, I've had friendship with benefits. Sooner or later one messes up the other."

"Is three weeks your idea of sooner? Or later?"

He laughed. "It's my idea of eternity if we're gonna keep this up."

"We're not. We're even." Her voice dropped to a notch above a whisper. "You took my chip, I take your point."

"I don't think so, but we'll see. Go take your shower." He tossed the duffel bag, and it slid across the floor until it hit the wall. "One of the benefits of my friendship: I'm one hell of a cook."

Chapter Six

When the call came from BLM Wild Horse Specialist Max Becker, Sally was filling out forms on the computer. Bureau forms begat Bureau calls, and Sally was not a fan of either. But Max was one of the good guys.

"So far, so good." His tone was heavy on *so far*. "Everybody I talk to likes your proposal for a trainers' competition. It falls right in line with some of our other incentive programs, and I know you'd do it up right. I'm a big Mustang Sally fan. But I just got another letter from somebody who isn't."

"Dan Tutan."

"Let's see. Yep. That would be him. Says you're letting the horses run wild." Max laughed. "Guess he's a comedian on the side. Anyway, he copied your congressional delegation and some lawyer, along with the Cattlemen's League and the governor of South Dakota."

"Threatening what? To sue me and the horse I rode in on?"

"To strike his magic match and hold some big feet to the flame until he gets me fired." He chuckled. "The horse I rode in on gets roasted over my coals."

"Are you scared?"

"Are you? This guy lives right down the road from you. Sounds like he's the kind who rams push into shove and takes credit for casualties."

"He's a dinosaur. They weren't green, were they? Tutan's not green. Kill, baby, kill. That's his motto."

"Well, I gotta tell you, Sally, there's a lotta people in the Bureau right now he can get to back his play. The district manager's going deaf from the miners and drillers screaming in one ear and the hunters and ranchers barking in the other. The rangeland management specialist rolls out his tri-colored, multiple-use spreadsheet, and before I know it, all those little boxes are filled up with test drills and grazing permits. He's got a few deer and antelope playing around in the margins, but there's no place to put my horses. They say we have to gather up another five hundred by the end of the summer. And I say..." He sighed wearily. "I say, give Sally Drexler's proposal a shot. And they say, *Shot? Euth injection, or is she talking guns?*"

"Are you serious?"

"You know I'm serious, and you know where I stand, but the squeeze gets tighter every day. All options are on the table, and that includes the one no horse lover wants to hear."

"They're protected," she insisted, but she knew the Wild Free-Roaming Horses and Burros Act had been challenged continually since 1971. With so many horses confined to holding facilities, the *free-roaming* part was becoming a joke. Some in Congress were saying that *protection* was just another word for nothing left to waste money on. A welfare program for wild horses they called it, and the horse was not an endangered species. "Where's *your* spreadsheet, Max?"

"Under my pillow."

Sally groaned. "Who's the comedian now?"

"That's all I've got going for me at one of those damn meetings. Guess I'm gonna have to break down and call the Video Professor about one of those free computer-training programs."

"I'll send you one. What else do I have to do to get the go-ahead on this project?"

"It would help if your neighbor would back off."

"What else?"

"I'm willing to work with you, Sally. I can appraise trainer applications with you, and I can set up the adoption after the competition is over. I'll be down in your area in a couple of weeks. You need sponsors."

"I have them." *Almost.* Zach's brother was going to contribute to the sanctuary. She hadn't asked him to sponsor the contest yet.

"Do you have enough help out there? I hear Little Horsin' Annie got hitched to that rodeo cowboy you had working for you. That's one way to reduce the payroll."

"And Zach brought a friend onboard. A farrier." Hank wasn't there at the moment. He'd left early yesterday for a rodeo not far from the Wyoming office Max was calling from, but he'd be back today. "A *volunteer* farrier."

"Now if we can just marry you off to a veterinarian," Max teased. "Your sanctuary is a little piece of horse heaven, Sally. I'm in your corner."

She felt so much better. Max Becker was in her corner. Damn Tootin' was calling in favors from his hunting buddies. And Hank Night Horse was on board with her for three weeks. Minus three days, and he was surely counting.

Maybe she could reason with Tutan. Compromise somehow. *Come on, Dan, let's share. Let's join forces and save the world.*

Not likely. Threatening him was more his speed. But with what? Letters, litigation, lawmakers. *It's who you know that counts.*

Sally was surrounded by people who counted. She was committed to a way of life, a legacy, a whole population of animals that counted. She was needed. *She* counted. Marrying her off to a veterinarian, doctor, lawyer or Indian chief would not make a difference in how much Sally Drexler contributed to the sanctuary.

She had work to do. Some of the horses would be tamed so that some could remain wild. *Wild.* Not kept alive in a holding pen. The sanctuary wasn't wilderness, and public land wasn't exactly open range, but it was a fair imitation of freedom. Sally had learned from the mustangs—you take your bliss where you find it, and you run with it when you can.

Tutan needed some tutoring on that particular point, but maybe Sally hadn't chosen the best way to go about it during their last meeting. She'd known the man all her life, and she'd never liked him. She'd been friends with his daughter, Mary, who had declared her freedom from her overbearing father by joining the army. She hadn't seen much of his shy, ever-cloistered wife since her friend left. Maybe Mary's mother could be recruited to her cause. Audrey Tutan was a gentle soul, and Sally knew she could gain her sympathy, which might count for something. Possibly a moratorium on complaints to the BLM. Maybe a purloining of letters.

Otherwise she would move to Plan B. She would

build a threat bomb. The components were yet to be determined.

Hoolie had all volunteer hands on deck for haying, which made it a good time for Sally to pay a visit to the Tutan ranch, especially since Dan was probably out in the field, too. Fresh off the call from the BLM, Sally was itching to try her hand at woman-to-woman diplomacy.

Trying her hand at driving was another matter. It had been a couple of years since she'd driven, but she was feeling good today. Good and irritated. She was powered up, and her mission wouldn't take long. She scanned the array of keys hanging on hooks in the mudroom. She decided she could handle Hoolie's little go-fer pickup. She'd be back before anyone knew she was gone.

Sally hadn't missed driving as much as she'd thought she would. She'd never told anyone, but there had been times when she'd scared herself when she was behind the wheel, even before her nervous system had started going haywire. She took it slow, kept the dust wake to a minimum, and reached the highway without incident. And why shouldn't she? Her vision in her left eye was better than what a lot of people could claim in both eyes put together. Five slow and easy miles up the road she drove through Tutan's fancy wooden gate.

Audrey Tutan answered her front door tentatively,

as though the sunlight was too strong or the air outside was too thick. She had always reminded Sally of a caged bird. Her hair had been white ever since Sally could remember, and she had always been fair in the face and thin everywhere—lips, hips, hands, voice. She looked confused as she peered from the shadows. "Dan isn't here right now."

Sally tipped her head to one side and smiled. *Remember me, Mrs. Tutan?* "I really came to see you."

"You did?" Audrey brightened as she drew the door back. "Well, that's very nice. Please come in, Sally. You're looking well. Dan said as much after he saw you at the wedding. I mean, when he stopped by the, um... He said Hoolie was the only one using a cane." Audrey caught herself. "I hope Hoolie's all right."

"He broke his ankle, but he'll be fine."

"Was it nice?" She closed the door. "Annie's wedding, I mean. Come sit with me. I'm all by myself today."

"It was lovely." Sally followed the tiny woman into the living room with its massive pine furniture and heavily draped windows. "Very small. Family, mostly."

"When you girls were all in school, we were like family." Audrey turned, took Sally's hand and drew her down beside her on the spruce-and-pinecone sofa. "I miss those days."

"I do, too. I miss Mary. Have you heard from her

recently? We were e-mailing regularly, but so much has been happening…"

"She must be okay." Audrey glanced away. "I would've heard otherwise."

"Time gets away from us, doesn't it?" Sally gave the bony, loose-skinned hand a slight squeeze. "Audrey, I don't understand why Dan is so completely opposed to what we've done with the Double D."

"He says it's hard enough to make a living raising cattle these days without competing with animal rights fanat—" she pressed her lips tight "—folks. You know how he is."

"You know me better than that, Audrey. I'm no fanatic, but I've always loved horses. So does Mary. She used to come over all the time, and we'd ride fence and check cows. The sanctuary is a dream come true for me."

"Dan says there's plenty of horses in the world."

"How do you feel about it?"

"I'm staying out of it. He's getting older. The kids are gone. I've never been much help as far as the cattle operation goes." She shook her head slowly, a helpless gesture. "If Dan says the horses are a nuisance…"

"He's been complaining about us to the BLM. We're trying to expand the program, and he's been calling the district office in Wyoming and complaining about the people coming in and out, the horses, the fence, the way we manage just about everything."

Audrey withdrew her hand, twisted her head to the side and spoke into her shoulder. "He says you're moving in on his grass."

"It's not his grass," Sally said gently. "We're taking unadoptable horses out of crowded pens. We're giving older animals a place to live out their lives the way nature intended. Audrey, they used to slaughter them by the thousands."

"I remember."

"It could happen again." She lowered her voice. "There's talk of allowing them to be rounded up and sold for slaughter."

"I don't like to see animals suffer, but I don't know how I can help you, Sally. Dan doesn't talk to me about these things."

"I was hoping you might talk to him."

"It wouldn't matter what I said. Ranching is his life. He knows his business." Her eyes were empty. "The older we get, the less we talk."

Sally couldn't keep pressing. It was too much like throwing a stick for an old dog. For Audrey's sake, she was glad she had come, and she asked, *hoped* she would return the favor. But she knew it wouldn't happen.

Now she was eager to get home. Barreling down Tutan's gravel approach toward the highway, Sally thought about options for getting Damn Tootin' off her back. Call the law. Call Congress. Call the media.

Call…what time would Hank be home? *Back.* What time would he be…

She was homing in on the gatepost on the left side, favoring the left side, her good side. She missed the movement on the right, the pickup turning onto the approach from the far lane, her fuzzy lane. There it was, left. Wheel hard right. Clutch, brake—leg? Leg! *Crunch.* Engine, killed. Gatepost? *Bull's-eye.*

Alive? *Check.* Conscious? *Must be.* Hurt? *Stay tuned.*

"What the hell are you trying to do?"

Tutan.

Rewind. Over and out.

"Are you all right?"

The last thing Sally wanted to see was that fat red face, but she carefully turned her head to the left anyway. Sure enough.

"I think so." She felt around the inside of the door for the handle.

"You better be sure. You wrecked your truck."

"Hoolie's truck."

"Did you break anything?"

"Hoolie's truck."

"I'd better call for help."

"Just let me…" She couldn't see much, but a roaring engine, screeching brakes and flying gravel were distinctive sounds. Had the two-lane highway become the scene of a demolition derby?

So was the voice calling for "Hoolie?"

Hank!

"It's not Hoolie," Tutan shouted. "I don't think she's hurt."

"Don't touch her. Sally?"

"This seat belt is a piece of crap." She hoped she sounded disgusted. She wasn't ready to look up and let him see the face of a rattled klutz.

"Take it easy. Do you hurt anywhere?" He reached through the side window and touched the side of her neck. "Your head?"

She closed her eyes and let relief wash over her. "I can't feel…anything…"

"Nothing? How about—"

"She's not even supposed to drive, for God's sake. Look what she's done." Red face, red voice. *Red filled her head.* "With her medical problems? I don't know what you people think you're doing, letting this girl get behind the wheel."

"Stay out of the way, Tutan." Hank opened the driver's side door. "Sit, Phoebe."

"Phoebe?" Sally whined. The dog answered in kind.

"She's okay, Phoeb. Tell her, Sally."

"I'm okay, Phoeb. Nothing hurts. I mean, I don't think I'm—"

"Is she bleeding? Anything broken? That's all you need on top of your MS, Sally. You almost hit me."

"*I will hit you* if you don't back off." Hank slid his

arms under her legs and behind her back. "See if it hurts to put your arms around my neck. Slow and easy, okay? You tell me if you feel the slightest…"

"You were outta control, Sally. I don't know what you're doing over here, but you coulda just called. Your father was my friend." The red voice followed, but Sally kept her face tucked against Hank's shoulder. "How long is that thing gonna be sittin' here?" the red voice demanded from a faraway place.

"I'm taking care of her first," Hank said. "If that *thing* ain't here when I come back for it, I'll be looking for you."

"Look what she did to my gate!"

"Which way should we go?" Hank looked up and down the highway, but he was running a checklist in his mind. No blood, bruises, bumps, breaks. He was pretty sure she hadn't been injured, but *pretty* was the operative word.

"You know the way home," she said quietly.

"I don't know the way to your doctor. Did you hit your head? That's the main thing."

"I lost my head. I do that sometimes." She paused. "Sometimes I need a good thumping."

"Well, you got one." He laid two fingertips on the signal-light switch. He was feeling impatient. "If you're not gonna tell me where to find your doctor, I'll go with my best guess."

"Which one do you want? My GP? My neurologist? My—"

"North or south?" he clipped. "Let's start there."

"South," she said. She reached into the backseat, where she got a hand-licking from an ally. "Take me home. I think I'm okay, but if not, I trust you."

He stepped on the brake and turned to her, scowling. "I don't know whether you're lyin' to both of us or just me, but trust me on this. I'm not taking you anyplace that doesn't have an X-ray lab."

"North."

He pulled into the highway and stared straight ahead. Yes, he'd heard. Yes, he knew what MS was. Basically. Questions? Comments? Not without an invitation from Sally.

But for Sally, there was nothing more to say. She'd blown her chance at three weeks of let's pretend by acting stupidly for one day. She glanced at the dashboard clock. *One hour* out of one day. He probably would have guessed before her time was up, but it was too soon. If she hadn't pushed, she could have been normal for a while longer. She could have deluded herself almost completely during this remission. Maybe it was over. Maybe her body had beaten the disease or at least found a way to hold it in check. Maybe she would actually live the scene she'd imagined so many times—the one where she was surrounded by cheerful people wearing white, proclaiming miracles. People, not angels. *It could happen.*

No. What could have happened—up until an hour ago—was a lovely three-week affair with a man who didn't look at her and hear a voice in the back of his head saying, *Don't forget, she's incurable.*

Hank waited in a chair outside one of the small, rural clinic's three exam rooms. Phoebe lay at his feet.

MS. So that was it. He should have known. *Would have* known if he'd been halfway objective. *Damn Tootin'.* Damn Tutan for telling him. He'd wanted Sally to tell him. Trust him. *Come clean,* he'd said, as if whatever she was keeping from him was something dirty. *Dirty secrets.* What other kind would a person want to keep?

From the beginning, objectivity hadn't been an option with Sally. He'd stayed out of the water, but that didn't mean he hadn't gone under. He knew the signs. He'd been there before. The trick was not to fight it. If you let go, you were supposed to be able to float. So he'd heard. Now that they were on par with each other in the personal-history department, maybe they could explore the options she'd laid out on the table. She wanted a friend. She needed certain benefits.

He was her man.

When the door opened, he almost jumped to attention.

"Dr. Bergen says I'm fine."

"That isn't exactly what I said." The doctor adjusted her wire-framed glasses. "I don't see any injuries except a bump on the head and probably some back strain, although Sally says it's nothing. She tells me you're a PA. You'll be around for a while?"

"I'm helping out at the ranch."

"The sanctuary," Sally said. "Hank's taking a working vacation. He's sort of an experiment. If he gives us a good review, I'm going to offer that as a volunteer option on our Web site." She glanced at Hank. "I'm working on a Web site."

The gray-haired woman gave an appreciative nod. "I could go for something like that. I've always wanted to volunteer for Doctors Without Borders, but this place can't spare me for more than a few days at a time."

"Rural clinics are hurting for staff," Hank said.

"Hank just got back from a rodeo. He patches up cowboys for a living, so he can still—"

"Did you take any X-rays?" he asked.

"None indicated." Dr. Bergen eyed Sally as though she might have missed something. "You're not experiencing any numbness now, right? Other than the vision in your right eye, which you were having problems with before the accident." Back to Hank. "Any sign of concussion, bring her back right away. How long have you been a rodeo medic?"

"Seven years."

"Well, then, you've probably had almost as much

experience with injuries like this as I have. Of course, multiple sclerosis complicates things a bit."

"I don't suppose you've run into too many cowboys with MS." Sally gave him her Sally-go-round-the-roses look.

"You're my first."

"Good." She smiled at the doctor. "We never forget our first."

"Make an appointment to see your neurologist as soon as you can get in. You're good to go." Dr. Bergen waved a business card she'd been palming all along. "This is where I'll find the Web site?"

"As soon as we launch it. If you know any veterinarians, we're always looking for volunteers."

Sally's limp was more noticeable as the three of them headed for the pickup, sitting there with the front tire kissing the curb and the back end a good three feet away. *Somebody* had sure been in a hurry.

"I like your style, Sally." He opened the door for her and offered her a hand, thinking his style wasn't too shabby, either. She questioned him with a look— like maybe she could read his mind about the way she walked—and she grabbed the door handle and hauled herself up onto the running board. "The business card, the volunteer comment. Opportunity comes knockin', you're not afraid to jump."

"Opportunity must be jumped while the jumping's good."

He laughed as he let Phoebe in back. He buckled himself in while Sally picked up where she'd left off.

"In my case, while the jumpers are in good jumping order."

"Ah, Sally." He shook his head, chuckling. "You are the damnedest… Did you think it would matter to me that you have MS?"

"Hmm, how should I answer this question? I hope it matters. Or…" She drew herself up and turned to him with a perfunctory smile. "I *knew* it would matter. It matters to everybody. When I'm using a cane, sometimes a wheelchair, that's the first thing people see." She raised an instructive finger. "Maybe it throws them off, maybe it doesn't, but that's who I become. And it's less than I am, and I get tired of waiting for them to catch up to me. When I'm having myself a nice little remission, why should I tell people? Especially people who won't be around that long."

Good question.

"Maybe because some people don't know what to make of all this jumping." He plugged the key into the ignition, shrugged, gave her a look that was probably more sheepish than he intended. "Some of us are scared spitless when it comes to jumping."

"Not you." Her eyes softened. "You were ready to jump when you thought I'd fallen in the lake."

"I wasn't thinking."

"But you've been thinking ever since. Thinking,

there's something wrong with this woman. Can't quite figure out what it is, but…"

"Not wrong. Risky. I like to know what I'm getting into. The ol' look-before-you-leap routine."

"You already looked!"

"Yeah, I did. And I was goin' for it." He gave a mid-forehead salute. "I had the image fixed in my mind."

"You saw yourself swimming?"

"Hell, no." He smiled. *Honey, cut me some slack.* "I saw myself giving you mouth-to-mouth."

"Now you tell me. I would have thrashed around and swallowed some water for you. Right, Phoebe? I've never had a water rescue." She returned his smile. "Your Damn Tootin' rescue was beautifully executed. Nice entry. Perfect timing. Thank you for that."

"It would've been sweet to put my fist through his face."

"I know." She dropped her head back on the headrest and stared at the ceiling. "How much damage did I do to Hoolie's pickup? I wish I could get it fixed before he sees it." She smacked her forehead with the heel of her hand. "Stupid."

"Don't beat yourself up." He reached for her smacking hand. "You can't help being a woman driver."

She raised her brow and smiled sweetly. "I guess not. If you like, I can teach you how to parallel park."

Chapter Seven

Hank had been the perfect gentleman. He had seen her to her bedroom door, asked about a heating pad, brought her cold packs and Sleepytime tea, and gone to the front door to answer Hoolie's "Where the hell's my pickup?" On his way out, he'd suggested a warm bath, even offered to fill the tub. She'd thanked him, said she'd take it from there knowing full well she was doing no such thing. She was letting him answer for her, and she was shamefully content to do so.

But she indulged herself with bath salts and a few bubbles. Why not? It was what she did best. Overextend, underperform. She wasn't hurting much—she'd never claimed she was—but water was always wonderful. *Feel while the feelin's good.* She laid her head back, closed her eyes and soaked it up.

Sally didn't need sight or sound—the door made no noise—when she was hooked into feeling. When the feeling was good, she felt change. New electricity, energy, presence. Manpower. She opened her eyes and smiled.

He wore black jeans. Nothing more. She hoped.

She drew a deep breath and sat up. Foam cascaded over her breasts, tickling her imagination. *Don't look now, but we are hot.* "I'm sorry you didn't catch me doing something more interesting."

"I'm not here to watch."

But he was. Something interesting was happening in the tub, and he was fascinated. He closed the door behind him without looking anywhere else.

"You came to play?"

"Brought you a bath toy." He plunged his hand in his pocket and pulled out a foil packet. "Rubber duck."

"Is that your bath toy of choice?"

"It's the one that's gonna float your boat."

She shrieked with delight as he stepped into the tub, jeans and all. Water sloshed onto the floor, bubble islands rocked back and forth. She drew her knees up to make room, but he took hold of her ankles, straightened her legs and wrapped them around his waist.

"I don't see how." She wiggled her bottom—a hen

getting comfortable in a flooded nest—and stroked his beautiful, brawny shoulders.

"You'll figure something out." His smiling eyes plumbed the depths of hers, tempting a little, teasing a lot. "You wanna get into my jeans, woman, you're gonna work for it."

"While you—"

"—find out what you taste like." He ducked as he slipped his hands around her, thumbs tucked into her armpits, lifting her until her nipple touched his lips. He brushed her so slightly, made her wind up so tightly that she almost interfered. But she held on, and he made it worthwhile with his nibbling lips and the barest tip of his flickering tongue and the warm whisper of his breath. "Sweet cakes with foam." He smiled against her nipple. "Which has a bite to it." He suckled, and then chuckled as he teased with his nose. "Not the kind I was hoping for."

"Sorry," she whispered.

"I don't mind swallowing."

"My kind of man." She buried her fingers in his hair. "You'll come out…smelling like a rose."

He grew and stirred beneath her. "Only for you."

She used his hair to ease his head back until his lips were within reach of hers, and then she kissed him. His thumbs toyed with her breasts, and their tongues played tag. He trailed fingers down her side, over her belly, between her legs and teased her most sensitive flesh until she thought she would die for want of him inside her. But he permitted only the edge of madness and not the full measure. It was at once excruciating and exhilarating, too bright to keep and too fine to let go. She closed her eyes, sheltered them against his neck, and gave herself over.

"Not fair," she whispered when the shuddering subsided.

He turned his mouth to hers and kissed her kindly. He was big and hard beneath her, fit to bust his zipper. She tightened her seat and rolled her hips slowly, raising wants and making waves. His kiss turned hungry, and he tasted every part of her mouth, but he couldn't seem to get his fill. He groaned. "Not fair."

She reached for the soap bottle, pumped a dollop into her palm, rubbed her hands together and lathered him—shoulders, arms, chest. She laughed when her turnabout with his nipples had him sucking air through his teeth. She took the measure of his rib cage, his flat belly, belly button, jeans button. Beneath the bath water it came undone easily. She hoped he would not.

He stilled her hand, poised on the zipper tab. "If I get caught in the teeth, it's all over."

She slipped her hand into his pants, becoming his protection. The tip of his penis pushed against the heel of her soapy hand. She smiled. *This puppy wants out.* She inched the zipper down. "Lift up."

"We're at T minus ten, honey. Any more *up* and it's *liftoff*."

"Hips, silly."

He braced his arms on the sides of the tub and lifted. And when she had his jeans down, she lowered her face into the water and took advantage of his precarious position, just for a moment. Just for a bit of pleasure he would not soon forget. The limited-time offer ended when the breath she could no longer hold became bubbles. He gave a pained laugh as she rose over him like Nessie, pushed her hair back and settled on his lap with an added bonus. It was hard to tell who was torturing whom as he opened the condom and she put it on him, but the pleasure that followed was mutual.

They stepped out of the tub into almost as much water as they left behind. They dried each other with thick bath sheets and traded more kisses and dove into her bed for more exploration and discovery. Every nerve in Sally's body was on high aler.. None slept. None missed the smallest trick.

And, oh, from head to toe, she felt wonderful.

"Tell me how you feel." He braced up on his arm and rested his head on his hand. Moonlight streamed through the window with cool night air and cricket calls. He smoothed her hair back from her forehead, his fingertips barely brushing the bump above her eyebrow. Marble sized. Not a shooter, but not a pee-wee either. Big and hard enough to give him concern.

"Happy." Her eyes were closed. Her mouth formed a soft crescent. "Drained and dreamy."

"How 'bout a massage?"

"Mmm…later." She turned toward him, tucked her whole body into him. "How about a snuggle?"

"I'm not letting you go to sleep yet."

"Why not?"

"I'm not ready."

She looked up, eyes wide with mock shock. "What kind of a man are you?"

"You have to ask?"

"Oh, that's right." Her eyes drifted closed, and that sweet, satisfied smile returned. "The doctoring kind."

"I'm not a doctor."

"And it's a good thing. I really don't like doctors." She laid her hand on his chest. "Play doctors, yes. Real doctors, no."

"How's your head?"

"I told you. Drained and dreamy."

"If you fall asleep, I'll just have to wake you up." His thumb grazed the knot on her head. "Still the same size."

"I have other bumps you can play with." She claimed his hand, drew it down and held it against her breast. "When you touch them you make them feel much bigger."

He chuckled. "You're the damnedest woman I've ever met."

"I think so, too, sometimes. I get all tucked up inside, and I—"

"*Tucked* up?"

"That's what I said, Henry. Tucked up." Clutching his hand in both of hers, she turned to her back and scooted up against him, like a small creature seeking shelter from the wind or shade from the high-plains sun. "I sort of suck myself inward. I become a prune, and I imagine myself screaming, 'Come on, you demons, try to take a piece of me now.' But I don't. I stay quiet and still, and I focus on getting through the next breath. I think that's what it's like to be damned."

"Me, too. It's not burning. It's drowning."

"And it's not painful. You know you're damned when you don't feel anything."

"I don't know about that. I've seen—"

"I do," she insisted. And then softly, "I do know. When you can't feel, you'd take anything. A hot poker. A wrecking ball." She drew a deep breath, and then let it go quickly. "Oh, I shouldn't say *I know.* Only part of me doesn't feel sometimes, and it comes back. It always comes back. I don't claim to know what it's like not to feel anything at all." She pressed his hand tight to her breastbone, and he uncurled his fingers and felt her heartbeat in the hollow of his palm. "I'm not a drama queen. I promise."

"I promise to stop calling you the damnedest woman, and we'll leave it there."

"No, no, then I'd be just another damned woman. One of your many damned women. If I'm the damnedest one you know, I'm queen of something. Queen of the damned, that's me." She stretched, full body, like a cat. "I'm not giving up the damnedest title without a fight. The next damned woman comes along, you can't call her *damnedest* unless she can take the crown from my cold, dead hands."

He laughed. "God, you're beautiful."

"I love your hands. They feel cool."

"They do? Maybe that's why you feel so nice and warm."

"I always do. It's part of the package." She looked up at him. "So now—I've avoided it as long as I can— the dreaded question."

"What's that?"

"Did you have to tow Hoolie's pickup? What did he say when he saw it? Was he—I'm such a coward— did he think it could be fixed?"

"That's three dreaded questions." One mental sigh of relief after another. "Starting with number two— because this really says it all—he wanted to know about you. Where were you, how bad were you hurt, had you seen a doctor, and all like that. As for question number one, the pickup started right up, and we took off before the devil knew we were there. We got back, he wanted to know what you were doin' over there. I said, damned if I know. I was just goin' down the road and saw his C10. Damn good thing you stopped, he said, and I said amen to that."

"You sound just like him."

"Is that a bad thing?"

"There's only one Hoolie," she said firmly, as though he thought otherwise. "What about question number three?"

"I know it can be fixed, but if it'll keep you awake for a while, you can keep worrying."

She smiled big. "One Hoolie, one Hank. One Little Henry, one medium-size Henry, one big beautiful Henry. I'm blessed."

"So much for queen of the damned."

"Damned crown's giving me a headache, anyway."

"As long as it's not me." He kissed the bump on her forehead. "Got that? I don't wanna be anybody's headache."

"I don't either. Let's make a pact." She lifted her chin. "Let's kiss on it."

Sally turned Hank down for breakfast. All she wanted to do was sleep. He decided to give her a couple of hours before checking up on her one more time, and then he'd get after Tutan's damn gate. He'd have it fixed good as new, maybe better, and then he'd welcome the criticism, the complaints, hell, the lawsuit. Bring it on. Sooner or later he'd give Damn Tootin' the tuning up he deserved. He hadn't figured out just what form it would take, but there would be a suitable settlement. But for now, Tutan's property would be repaired.

Hank found Hoolie and Kevin in the machine shop, their heads under the hood of the C10, which they'd driven back from the scene of the accident without incident. Hank stationed himself on the third side of the male-bonding altar. A pickup engine was as good as a campfire.

Maybe better.

"Yep," Hoolie said, "she's gonna be good as new, soon as her replacement parts come." He patted the dented fender tenderly. "I've already found the headlamp housing and this whole quarter panel on the Internet."

Hank acknowledged the find with a raised brow.

"You search the Internet much? Any tool you can think of for shoeing horses, you just put the words in the box...." Two bony index fingers proudly demonstrated on the air keyboard. "You want the good stuff, put the word *vintage* in there somewhere. Press Enter, and here they come. Like cake, like pie. You ever play Scavenger Hunt?"

"Nope." Hank glanced across the man-bonding pit at Kevin. "You?"

Kevin shrugged. "Sounds like what I got arrested for last year."

"You gotta learn the rules of the game, boy. The tricks of the trade. You should see all my bookmarks. You scavenge around on the Internet, you can buy and sell, you can trade, you can—"

"Snag yourself a rich widow," said Kevin. "Come on, Hoolie, I've seen you friending the women on Facebook."

Hoolie folded his arms. "No harm in exchanging e-mails with females."

"You want the good stuff, you leave out the word *vintage,*" Hank said.

"The best e-pal is a gal with a little age on her," Hoolie advised. "If she asks for pictures before the third message, one of us is swingin' on the wrong porch."

"How's Sally?" Kevin asked Hank.

"I kept her up all night, so she's sleeping in this morning. She hit her head. She's got a goose egg the size of your *pahsu.*"

"His what?"

"Nose," Kevin said. "And mine ain't that big, so it's no excuse to keep her from getting her rest."

"I see a lotta concussions. You let her go to sleep too soon, she might not wake up."

"Hank's halfways a doctor," Hoolie told Kevin. "Physician's practitioner, they call it."

"Physician's assistant," Hank amended.

"What was she doing over at Tutan's?" Hoolie asked. "Did she say?"

"We didn't get into it." Hank leaned his forearms on the fender and admired the old six-banger engine. "She feels real bad about the damage on this baby."

"She, uh…she's a terrible driver."

"I know she has MS." He said it quietly, without looking up. "Tutan was turning into the approach, and they nearly collided. She couldn't work the pedals. 'Course he pitied her for having MS and ripped into her for driving." He glanced across the engine at Hoolie. "She coulda told me herself."

"We don't talk about it unless she…you know. It's for her to decide. Lately she's been…you'd never know unless…"

"Unless somebody told you." Hank nodded. Pride. He knew what that was like. "The leases she's trying to get, the horse-training challenge, she's pretty determined."

"That's Sally for you."

For *him?*

Hell, it had nothing to do with him. Sally was determined to be Sally. She'd honed the edge on her defensive game long before he came along. Which was understandable. Nothing personal, which was good. Under the circumstances, friends with benefits probably made perfect sense, especially since he wouldn't be around long.

"What's it gonna take?" Hank straightened his back, braced his hands on the pickup fender. "More people, money, connections, what?"

"Yeah, all that and maybe a guardian angel. I don't think she oughta be takin' so much on. Zach and Annie don't know the half of it." Hoolie smiled. "Sally's the one who got the sanctuary started. I didn't think much of the idea at first. Now I can't imagine a better one."

"She's supposed to make an appointment with her neurologist. I'd like to be the one to take her."

"I'd offer you my pickup, but…"

"We'll take mine. I'll take the topper off and leave it in the shop if it won't be in the way. About everything I own is in it."

"No problem," Hoolie said.

"We might be gone overnight. You never know. Can you handle—"

"'Course we can." Hoolie eyed Hank anxiously. "She's okay, isn't she? She's just getting double-checked, right?"

"Yep. When you're special, you see a specialist." Hank rapped his knuckles on the fender. "Right now, I've got some repairs to make on Tutan's front gate."

"I'll go with you," Kevin said eagerly.

"I need you here." Hoolie had cold water for Kevin, heated advice for Hank. "Don't let him push you around. Sally had a good reason for goin' over there. Whatever it was."

"You think he'll try to push me?" He could only hope.

"No. He ain't that stupid."

"Unfortunately." Kevin was greatly disappointed.

* * *

Hank tried the Tutans' doorbell, but there was no sound. He knocked on the door. Either way, it was a formality. If there was anyone home, they'd seen him coming a mile away. He gave a full minute before turning to leave. The door whined softly, a tentative opening, slight shape in the shadows.

"I'm looking for Dan Tutan. The name's Hank Night Horse. I'm helping out over at the Double D."

"Night Horse?" It was a woman's voice.

"I'm a friend of Zach Beaudry's. I came to fix the front gate."

"Oh." The door opened, and a small, mostly gray lady emerged. She wore a blue shirt and tan pants, but everything else about her seemed gray. "Dan's out cutting hay. How's Sally? Is she home?" She hung on to the doorknob with one hand and the door frame with the other, but she seemed hesitant, like she was trying to decide whether she should try to block an end run or step aside and let him score. "I was going to call, but I didn't want to cause any upset."

"I took her to the clinic. No injury to speak of."

"Tell her I hope she's…" She dropped her gaze along with her left hand. She looked defeated. "Tell her I'm sorry."

"Sorry for…"

"Upsetting her. I know stress causes those spells sometimes, where she loses control over her legs or something. All she wanted me to do was talk to him."

"Talk to your husband?"

"He's got his side, too. Who's to say?" The thought of two sides seemed to buck her up some. "Tell you the truth, I wish he'd cut back on the cattle. We don't need a big operation anymore. He's got nobody to take over for him. Kids are gone. They've got their own lives. But…" She gave an open-handed gesture, a sigh. "Sally was my daughter Mary's best friend."

"Sally stopped by to visit with *you,* then."

"Hardly ever see her anymore. She's like me— doesn't get out much, especially in the winter."

"She's completely dedicated to the horses. She wants to get along. She was just hoping you'd put a good word in your husband's ear."

"It wouldn't make any difference. He doesn't want to give up those grazing permits, plus the Indian land. He has some influence with…important friends, I guess you could say."

"It doesn't hurt to have important friends."

"Or *any* friends. We all need friends." She frowned. "Dan didn't say anything about you coming to fix the gate."

"He said a little something *to me* about the gate. You can tell him I came by with materials and offered to fix it like it was."

"Are you…?" She gave him a quizzical look. "Did you know John Night Horse? He used to work for us." He stood uncomfortably for her scrutiny. It surprised and almost disappointed him when she shook her head. "No, that was a long time ago. You would have been a child."

"I would have been twelve."

"He was related to you, then." She gave him a moment to make his claim, and when he offered none, she looked relieved. "He was a good man. I don't think they ever really found out what happened. But he was a good man."

Hank nodded. Like some TV prosecutor, he almost said, *no more questions.* Mrs. Tutan probably took most people for good, even though she was mostly a sad woman. Pumping her for information was like kicking a wounded animal. She clearly lived her life on a need-to-know basis. She didn't know what had happened to John Night Horse, didn't want to know. She hadn't told Tutan why Sally had come over, and wouldn't tell Tutan about Hank's call unless she was asked for some reason. She wouldn't want to cause an upset.

Hank had missed lunch. Sally was trying hard not to miss him, telling herself that last night he'd given her something she'd never had before, and that was all she wanted to think about now. Not the whys or the wherefores or whether it would happen again.

Replay the experience, Sally. Everything he said and did, everything you felt and felt and felt. Keep it alive inside, where nothing can take it away and you can have it over and over again, no matter what.

But she couldn't help watching the road while she watered the garden, listening for his pickup when she turned off the faucet. He'd gone to the neighbors' on a peace-making mission, which—given he had no real duty to any part of the Double D—was so far above the call it was almost saintly.

Whys and wherefores be damned, she waited. She watched and listened, and when she saw the flash of white on the highway, heard the rumble of the engine and felt the promise of having him back, she was content with whatever he was up to, as long as she was part of it. And she knew she was.

There was no we're-a-couple-now kiss when he met her in the yard. She could have offered, but she was tuning in to his cues, which went against all her instincts. She wanted to jump his bones and plant one on him. She made do with returning his glad-to-see-you smile and telling him she'd saved him some lunch.

He closed the back door behind them, grabbed her arm, turned her and drew her to him. His kiss brought last night forward. It was still with him, too. She clung to him and celebrated, trading kiss for kiss with equal satisfaction.

"How's your head?" He pulled back so he could get a look.

"All better."

He smiled wistfully as he measured the lump on her

forehead with his thumb. "Not quite, but you're still alive and kissing."

"You fixed Tutan's gate?"

"Not yet. He wasn't around, and his wife wouldn't give me the go-ahead. We tried, huh?"

She slipped her arm around his waist and walked him into the kitchen. "I have an appointment in Rapid City tomorrow. Hoolie says you're taking me."

"Makes sense, doesn't it?"

"Not if you're doing it because you're, you know…"

He laughed. "A halfways doctor?"

"Hoolie's a kick, isn't he?" She slid away, went to the refrigerator and took out the sandwiches she'd made for him. "I know that's the real reason Zach talked you into staying." She took a plate from the cupboard. "I didn't care then—I just wanted them to go on a honeymoon, for heaven's sake—but I wasn't planning to con you into being my personal halfway doctor. I don't want you to…" She turned to him, her hands, braced on the counter, bracketing her hips. "You don't need to be involved in my medical issues."

"Okay."

"That's not one of the benefits."

"Is there a list somewhere? I know our arrangement was pretty vague, but you start talkin' benefits, seems like there should be some negotiation."

"I'm serious, Hank. You were absolutely right—you're not the cure for what ails me. And I'm not your patient." She gave a shy smile. "I want to be something you don't already have."

"That covers a lot of territory." He lifted one shoulder. "I have friends. One or two, anyway."

"Women?"

"I know some women." His smile was slow and lazy. "None like you."

"That's nice. I like that. And I appreciate your offer to drive me to Rapid city. I just don't want you to feel like you have to—" she drew a deep breath and sighed "—take care of me."

"I don't feel like I have to do anything. What time is your appointment?"

"Nine." She perked up some. "And there's something I want to show you afterward. It's a little bit out of the way, but I really think it's important for you to see it."

"Out of the way in what direction?"

"North and east."

"Perfect. You show me yours, and I'll show you mine." He loaned her an actual smile. "I've got a few things to take care of at home."

"Cool! We'll take the high road to the day horses and the low road to the Night Horses."

"What's the quickest way for me to get to that food behind you?"

She returned his smile with interest. "The toll road."

Chapter Eight

"Mr. Night Horse?" The crisp voice jerked Hank out of his waiting-room-aquarium reverie. He blinked up at the red-haired, flourpaste-faced woman standing over him. "This way, please."

He followed the crepe-soled shoes and ample ass down a bright, narrow hallway. If she was taking him to a different part of the clinic, it probably wasn't a good sign. He imagined Sally "resting comfortably," tried to imagine what might have come up, what he could say or do to add to her comfort. Back to the friendship part of the bargain. He'd lied. He had more than one or two friends.

He'd told the truth. There was none like her.

The nurse rapped on the door before ushering him into a plush exam room. Specialists had it made.

This one was losing his dark hair a patch at a time, but he was letting the sides grow to compensate. He wore a crisp shirt and tie with his white coat, and he stood to gladhand Hank. "Sally's all set, doing just fine. She was telling me you're a rodeo medic. I have a friend who works with the Justin Sportsmedicine Team. Rod Benoit from Billings. Wondered if you've run into him."

"Dr. Benoit. Sure." Hank held a flat hand five feet above the floor. "Little guy with big hair. Crazy mustache."

"That's Rod. If he hadn't gone into medicine, he would've been a cowboy. He loves rodeo. Been pushing helmets and safety vests on bull riders for years."

"He's made a lot of headway." Hank chuckled. "So to speak."

"It's a good program. I see a lot of sports injuries. I know cowboys don't like to take off their hats except to eat or pray, but I'm a big supporter of helmets."

"Yeah, me, too."

"I just wanted to meet you. When Sally said she had a rodeo medic sitting out there in the waiting room, I told my nurse, I said, bring him on back."

Hank only had eyes for Sally, who was sitting in the corner, curiously quiet.

"Oh, she's fine," the doctor said. "Far as I can tell, none of her marbles fell out."

"So there's nothing…"

"She looks a lot better than the last time she was in. Well, except for her vision in that right eye, but that—"

"That's why I'm not driving." Sally sprang from the chair as though her name had been called.

"No, that's not why. That's not what caused the accident. We all have our limitations, and you know yours. You can't deny the disease, Sally." The doctor turned to Hank. "Tell Benoit Tony Schmidt said hello." He snapped his fingers. "Almost forgot." Schmidt took a folded check from his pocket, snapped it open with his thumb and handed it to Sally. "On my account."

With the door closed behind them, Hank turned to Sally. "*He* pays *you?*"

"He supports the sanctuary. I told him about the Wild Horse Challenge, and he wrote out a check." She gestured eagerly toward an exit sign at the end of the hallway. "We can go out this way."

"That nurse came to get me, I didn't know what was goin' on."

"He just wanted to meet you."

"And how did that come about?"

"He wanted to know how I got here. So I told him all about you." She turned to him as she leaned on the push bar of a side door. "What did you *think* was going on?"

"Hell, I thought something was wrong." He reached past her to lend his hand to their escape. "The way the nurse said, 'This way, please.' And then Dr. Tony's quizzing me like he's checkin' out my credentials."

"He thinks what you do is pretty cool. He says it's become a highly specialized field since I was involved as a stock contractor. There aren't that many of you, and I'm monopolizing an important team member."

"He said that?"

"*I* said that." She was on the march to his pickup, and he noticed her limp was more pronounced. "He said the part about you being such a rarity, and I just said…" He clicked the remote to unlock the door while she stood with her back to him. "I didn't say anything. Do they think I'm a child? A helpless, hopeless…" She jerked on the door handle. "I hate being talked around."

Hank knew what she meant. Talked down to, talked around, ignored. It was no way to treat people. He laid his hand on her shoulder. "You're not the kind to put up with it, either."

She turned her head, scowling. "What's that supposed to mean?"

"It means we're both rarities. Some people don't know how to act around us." He reached for the door handle, but she hung on. "Let me show you how a cowboy treats a lady." She hung on still. "An *Indian* cowboy. Rare as hen's teeth."

Her scowl melted. Her hand gave way to his claim

to the privilege of opening the door. He wanted to kiss her right out there in public, but he figured the way she was looking at him, the way he felt looking at her said it all without letting anyone else in.

"Hank," she said, just when he was ready to roll. "I also think what you do is pretty cool. It's way more important than repairing busted gates and driving me around."

"I just came back from an event in Wyoming. I call my own shots. I think you know that." He stopped at the street corner. *Yield, shift gears, move on.* "So, I'm calling on you to call our next turn. We're headed east on thirty-four? How far?"

Forty miles east of town, she showed him her second-worst nightmare. She asked him not to stop the pickup, but to slow down and take a good look at the two hundred "unadoptable" horses warehoused on a few acres of land owned by a private contractor. They had been rounded up by helicopter and removed from public land where they were supposed to be left to roam freely. One by one the unattractive, unhealthy, uncooperative and otherwise unlucky creatures that had passed their sell-by date turned sad eyes toward the road. These were some of the horses an expanded Double D sanctuary would accommodate.

"If all goes well," Sally said, more to the faces in the field than the man who had her back.

The edgy growl of the pickup's big engine echoed Hank's feeling. He'd heard about the holding facilities, but he hadn't seen one. "Why can't we stop?" This crawling along the shoulder of the road was not how he rolled. "Are we being watched? Through a rifle scope, maybe?"

"You have to admit, I add considerable excitement to your life."

"Hell, you're a walk in the park."

"Didn't you notice that sign back there?"

"Which one?" He was looking for a gate.

She turned to him, all cocky, giving him that *what-of-it?* look. "I'm practically blind in one eye, but I'm pretty sure it said Stay in Your Car."

"Oh, *that* sign." And *that* Sally. The unsinkable one. "That was just the top line. The practically blind line. The twenty-twenty line said, Entering Sioux Indian Country."

"It did not."

"The next one will. Watch your picnic basket. If they smell food, you're in real trouble."

She smiled for him, her eyes gleaming, defying deficiency. "You keep the engine running while I open the gate."

He laughed. "I was thinkin' the same way."

"Which is why we can't stop." She turned to the window. "Hang in there," she told the watchers. "We'll be back." And to Hank, "Won't we?"

How had he missed it? It was always the eyes that got to him—somebody looking to him to toss her a bone or toss him in the air, to take away her trouble or take away his pain. The eyes had it, said it, got to him and stayed with him long after his were closed for the night. More each day he was finding himself lost in Sally's eyes, but somehow he'd missed her loss. It was physical, and he was all about *physical*. As long as he didn't see any medical problems, she didn't have any. Right? He was the doctor. *Halfway*.

But he could have sworn she saw him clearly. Whether she accepted what she saw as what she got was another matter, *her* matter.

So, what the hell was the matter with him? If this was a classic case of the blind leading the blind...

He put his foot down. The pickup leaped onto the blacktop, engine roaring on the front end, tires kicking gravel out the back.

"It's only one eye, you know," she said.

"What?"

"My right eye's been sucky lately, but I have X-ray vision on the driver's side. I can see the wheels turning in your head. What are we doing?"

"Damn if I know." Getting away from a gate he couldn't open, pain he couldn't touch, eyes he wouldn't forget. "Tutan has friends in high places. I've got relations in all kinds of places. You're gonna meet my sister-in law."

* * *

Sally had been sleeping. She hadn't meant to, but Hank had gone silent on her, and she'd dozed off. Her mouth had probably exposed still more of her less-than-appealing side by falling open. When she opened her eyes, she saw tall grass in myriad shades of green and tan carpeting mile after mile of rolling plains. Buffalo grass it was called, but it fed horses just as well. Cattle, too, but they were relative newcomers. Before the cattle and the cattlemen, all of it had been Indian Country. Hank pointed out a sign that did, indeed, declare that they were entering the small portion that was left. South Dakota buttes and badlands softened into hills and bluffs as they traveled north.

The Night Horse place was tucked into the hills. In a suburb it would have been called a tract house. Here it was a "scattered site"—a modest home without neighbors. Cattle and a few horses grazed the hillsides. A few cottonwood trees, a small swing set, a couple of cars and a vegetable garden filled the yard.

A slightly shorter, somewhat heavier version of Hank without the cowboy hat emerged from the front door as Hank and Sally closed the pickup doors.

"Back so soon, brother?"

"I smelled frybread."

Sally inhaled deeply. Hot lard, sage smoke and tomato plants.

"Where's Phoebe?"

"She's hangin' with friends." Hank turned, winked at Sally as she approached. Either that or he was squinting into the sun. She chose the wink. "Sally, my little brother, Greg."

"Is this that Sally you were talking about?" Greg's eyes had a quicker sparkle than his brother's. Quick and sweet, as opposed to slow and killer. "Look at her smile. Yeah, he's been talking you up."

"You told your doctor about me, I told my big-mouth brother about you," Hank confessed. "I guess that means something, huh?"

"It means you're a fast worker when you put your mind to it." Greg punched his brother's shoulder. "We've got fresh frybread and *wojapi*. Come and eat."

Kay Night Horse welcomed Sally to her kitchen with a glass of wild mint tea and a chair next to the counter. Golden-brown squares of bread were piled high in a cardboard box next to a huge iron skillet on the stove. Steeped mint and steamy fruit scents mingled with deep-fat frying and yeast.

Sally nodded toward the oil-stained box. "I can tell that's the fresh frybread, but Greg mentioned canned something, and it smells like berries."

"Juneberries," Kay said. "Dried from last year. We're a couple of weeks away from fresh. Don't you pick juneberries?"

"I wouldn't know a juneberry from a june bug. My sister offers wild-plum jam to any of her students who'll bring her the plums. Annie's a wonderful cook."

"Sally's sister teaches at Winter Count Day School," Hank said. The men had taken chairs at the table. "Isn't that where you went to school, Kay?"

"For a year, but then I went to Pierre. How long has your sister been there?"

"Five years. She's younger."

"Sally and her sister turned their ranch into a home on the range for wild horses." Hank nodded as Kay set a glass of tea on the table in front of him. "Since there's already a Home on the Range for Boys, they call it the Double D Ranch."

Sally caught Greg looking doubtfully at her chest. "My father's name was Don Drexler. My *grand*father's name was Don Drexler." She laughed. "We do get some strange calls when we advertise for volunteers."

"What did this guy say?" Greg wanted to know. Hank whacked the back of his brother's head, and everyone laughed.

More animated than she'd yet seen him, Hank described the wild-horse sanctuary and the need to expand it. He had the air of a man on his home turf, but he kept Sally center stage. She was Mustang Sally, Snow White and St. Francis rolled up into one. And he was just the man to hook her up.

"Does the name Tutan ring a bell, little brother?"

Greg gave the name a moment's pause. "Was that the

guy who owned the ranch where the old man was killed?"

Hank nodded. "He's Sally's neighbor. He's also her main opposition. There's some remote country west of Sally's place that should be part of that sanctuary. It's prime for mustangs. Nobody would ever bother them. Some of it's tribal land." He raised his voice toward the kitchen. "Do you still have relatives on the council down there, Kay?"

"I've got one who generally looks out for the landowners, two who side with the Indian ranchers, and one who'll butt heads with anybody." Kay refilled Sally's glass. "Your neighbor leases Indian land?"

"Some." Sally held up her hand and whispered *thanks.* "If I can get those leases, I can get the grazing permits on the adjoining public land. We could accommodate twice as many mustangs."

Greg grinned. "What's in it for us?"

"Horses."

He laughed. "Looks like you've finally found a soul mate, brother. Did you show her your latest rescues? My brother's a soft touch when it comes to horses."

"They become part of who you are," Sally said. "They can lift a person off the ground—body, mind and spirit. They've been such wonderful partners for us for so long that we forget they were once wild. Like dogs and cats, domestic horses should have wild relatives. We must make sure of it. Some roots must be preserved, some seeds, some…"

She glanced at the brown faces, the brown eyes turned her way, and she could feel herself turning red. She lowered her gaze, studied the glass of pale tea. Wild mint. The scent of wild berries filled her nose. "We bring some of the horses in for people to adopt, to keep and use so that some can be left alone."

"Do you think they know?" Hank asked. "The one who doesn't get away, does he say to himself, I'll stand in a corral the rest of my life so my relations can run free?"

"I think so," Sally said hopefully. "I really do. And that's what we get out of the deal. We get to be with the ones who sacrifice. Maybe they can teach us something."

"Sure. If we can figure out how to learn."

"People adopt horses for their own use, but they go to all kinds of programs as well." Sally leaned into the discussion. "They're amazing, these horses. They're incredibly sensitive, and lend that sensitivity to us, in our lives…" She lifted one shoulder. "They've helped me."

"One of my cousins got in on a horse-training program in the prison in Nevada. It changed his life." Kay brought a plate of frybread and a bowl of hot fruit pudding to the table. "See if you like this, Sally. The missionaries taught us to make frybread, but the *wojapi* is what makes it really good, and that's ours."

Sally savored the food. It was almost as good as Annie's blueberry pie, which was to die for. As was the generous and gentle man who shared his family with her. He believed in her cause, and this was proof.

"I have to go pick up the girls from basketball camp," Kay told the group after taking a phone call. "They missed the bus again."

Sally started gathering dishes off the table. "May I ride along with you?" She glanced at Hank, who nodded and smiled.

Once the dusty, white Chevy was rolling on smooth blacktop, Sally turned from her polite questions about Hank's athletic nieces—questions eliciting little more than a word or two in response—to her real concern. "I don't mean to put you on the spot with your relatives on the Tribal Council. I don't usually ask for favors five minutes after I meet someone."

Kay didn't miss a beat. "How much time did Hank get?"

"Funny you should ask. Within the first five minutes, I think I did him a favor." She chuckled. "Of course, I could be flattering myself."

"First he's singing for some cowboy's wedding— he tried that song out for us, and *jeez* that was pretty."

"It was wonderful."

"And then he's helping this cowboy out for a few weeks, and then it's all Mustang Sally and Kay, can you help us out? I don't know what you did for him, but I hope it lasted more than five minutes."

Sally stared. She gave it at least five seconds. And then she burst out laughing. She had met her no-bull match in Kay Night Horse. When she caught her breath, she told Kay the skinny-dipping story, and they shared a good laugh.

"I'll do what I can for your sanctuary because Hank wants me to," Kay said. "If he says it's a good thing, then it is. What you said about the wild horses goes for Hank, too. He's helped a lot of people. The kind who won't let just anyone get too close."

"I know."

"That's the kind he wants to be. Tries to be. Lift a person off the ground, brush him off and send him on his way. You do that day after day, you keep your guard up, you should be fine."

"My, um…this friend who's a doctor, he was eager to meet Hank. He says—"

"He took care of Greg after their mother died. Hank was fifteen. They stayed with relatives, but Hank looked after his little brother. When Hank got into the Indians in Medicine program at the university, Greg stayed with him. Stayed with him for a while after Hank got married."

"Was he there when Hank's son was killed?"

"Greg was with me by then." Kay glanced at her as she slowed for a turn at a T in the road. "Deborah— Hank's wife—she was pretty and everything, maybe not as smart as she thought she was, but smart enough. It turned out she couldn't do real life. When that little boy died and that woman left, Hank's world caved in on him. But he's a survivor. He's the kind who picks himself up and goes at it again, only twice as hard as he was before. He'll turn himself inside out for you if that's what you want."

It wasn't. And he wouldn't. Kay had it all wrong. "We haven't known each other very long."

"Like I said, the way you talked about the horses, you could have been talking about Hank."

"Amazing," Sally whispered, thought about it, turned to Kay and smiled. "Did I use the word *amazing?*"

"Amazing he let you get close to him so quick."

"Don't worry. His guard is secure. And I'm harmless."

The look Kay gave said *we'll see.* But she smiled. "At least you come with some horses."

Nothing had been said about how long they would be staying or where they would be sleeping, but Hank and Sally sat outside on kitchen chairs as dusk fell and traded stories with Greg and Kay. Stars appeared and so did the guitars. In the old days, Hank said as he strummed, he and his little brother had often sung together for their supper. But those days were gone, Greg crooned as he tightened his E string. Now dessert would do nicely.

Sally was charmed by the music, mesmerized by the stars glittering against the black-velvet sky. When she saw flashes of color, she thought her bad eye was playing a good trick on her. Her senses were, after all, weirdly wired. Maybe she was hearing in color. She closed one eye at a time, and the stars danced for her, but the colors vanished.

Kay touched her arm and pointed. There it was again, a bit brighter, a little braver. Hank looked up, strummed a final chord, and grabbed Sally's hand. "Grand finale," he said as he pulled her out of the chair. "You guys comin'?"

"Can't." Greg hit a low note. "Kids."

Hank's pickup roared to the top of the steep hill behind the house. He cut the engine, and all seemed suddenly quiet. Cut the lights, and all was dark. He grabbed a couple of blankets out of the back, spread one over the crisp grass, and with a sweeping gesture offered Sally the best seat in the universe. A soft breeze rustled the grass, a few crickets held a powwow in the draw below, and a brigade of ghostly rainbows jostled in the northern sky.

"Northern lights," Sally whispered. "I haven't seen them since I was a girl."

"You're still a girl." He stretched out on his back and tucked his arms beneath his head.

"Oh, no, I'm not." She lay down beside him. "You need a woman."

"We used to come up here at night when we were boys. No girls. But you're right. We thought about women. Each of us got to pick one to bring up here. If we couldn't get that one, we'd be out of luck."

"Who did you pick?"

"Natalie Wood. I'd've had her for sure if she wasn't dead. Greg was gonna get Madonna. He wanted to see what was under those cones. I told him a woman who shows that much skin in public can't be trusted." He chuckled. "We were boys."

"Natalie Wood," she mused. She wondered what Deborah looked like. She wouldn't ask. *Natalie Wood* she could say aloud, but not *Deborah*. Deborah was not harmless.

He sat up. She woke up from her musing, looked up and followed his lead. One by one the lights were turning on—a battalion of vertical rainbows bobbing shoulder to shoulder to shoulder across the night sky. The colors were vivid, the palette complete. So vast was the sky, so enormous the display that it was impossible to be separate from it. Sally's vision cleared. Her body melted. She became blue-green. She ebbed and flowed with the swells of refracted light. She was beautiful.

She was flawless.

She touched Hank's arm, just to be sure he was still there. He put his hand on her thigh. So cool. She could feel it right through her jeans. Deliciously bracing, like springwater. Wherever the lights took them, they were going there together.

"Lie back," he told her when the lights began to recede. He unbuttoned her jeans, unzipped, unleashed his mouth and all its unsettling skills on her belly. He lowered her clothing, nibbled and tickled and tongued until all the colors of the rainbow rushed ahead of his painstaking advance on her sentient core. She could neither keep still nor silent. "Keep your eyes on the skies," he whispered. "Still there?"

"Yes." It was all she could manage. A single word for infinity fading too fast.

"Don't close your eyes yet." He kissed her high inside her thigh and low between her thighs. "Still?"

"Yes, but…"

"Close your eyes and open your legs for me," he whispered, his breath soft and stimulating. She could hardly move, and so he helped her. The lights were still there, and his tongue charged them up, more brilliant than before. Brighter than icy morning, more dazzling than sun through rain.

He caught her colorful thrills and delicate spills on his lips and delivered them to hers, let her taste her essence, which only made her crave his. They peeled each other bare and touched, tasted, breathed each other in until they blended so perfectly that her leading him to her and his going inside was inevitable.

They made their own rainbow.

Chapter Nine

The brown-and-white sedan with the word *Sheriff* emblazoned on the sides was the second most unwelcome traveler on the three-mile stretch of gravel between the highway and the Drexler house. Not that Sally had anything against Cal Jenner—she'd voted for him three times—but the news he brought almost always had something to do with the owner of the *most* unwelcome vehicle.

"You've got horses on the road again, Sally," Cal announced as he closed the door with the letters *S-h-e* behind him and hitched up his brown pants. "I don't see a gate open, don't see any fence down, but they're getting out somewhere."

"Kevin!" Hank beckoned with a gesture. The boy took the rubber ball from Phoebe's mouth, tossed it up and hit a pop fly into the shelter belt, sending both dogs on a tear before he dropped the bat and headed for home. "How far south?" Hank asked the lawman.

"They're actually about four miles north of here."

"I've been gone for a couple of days, just drove down that road not thirty minutes ago," Sally protested. "Somebody's messing with our fences."

"Probably some of your volunteers. Have you taken on any new recruits lately?"

"No, but even if we had they wouldn't be cutting our fences."

"I didn't see any sign of anything like that goin' on," Cal said. "You got any better ideas?"

"Well, let me think." Sally tapped her chin and rolled her eyes skyward.

Cal shook his head. "Dan hasn't complained to me in—I don't know—couple weeks at least. Now, I have heard from the BLM out there in Wyoming. They want to know how you're doing. I say, *how they're doing what?* And they say, how you're doing with the community. Which is a loaded question, and I'm trained to duck and cover."

Sally wasn't amused. "Are you getting reports on us from anyone else?"

"Nope."

"Then why are you ducking?"

"I admire what you're doing, Sally. You know that. I want to see the Sheriff's Posse go completely Spanish Mustang." Cal turned to Hank. "We've got braggin' rights to six adopted mustangs on the drill team now. I'll take them over any other horse in the bunch. The spirit of the old West lives in those horses. I'm all for—"

"You don't get any other complaints," Hank affirmed.

"An anonymous call once in a while. Horses on the highway. Usually there's nothing to it, but I always check it out."

"You mention that to the BLM?"

"If they ask."

Hank laid his hand on Kevin's shoulder. "There's some horses out on the right of way, a few miles north. Saddle up and run 'em across the road and through the west gate. Make sure that side's secure."

"In with the cattle?" Kevin asked.

"For now." Hank turned to Sally. "I'll have a look on the east side."

She nodded. "We keep our fence in good repair. You know that, Cal."

"Yours is better than most."

"Riding fence is everybody's favorite assignment around here." She glanced at Kevin, who was beating a path back to the barn, eager to carry out Hank's order.

"On the other hand," Cal added, "if horses are the spirit, cattle are the lifeblood of this part of the country."

"We have cattle, too. The Drexlers have been here longer than the Tutans. We've changed our focus." Sally divided her smile between the two men. "It used to be disappointing not to make any money ranching. These days we're *purposely* not making a profit."

"Somebody has to make enough profit to pay some taxes, or the county's got no way to gas up my squad car." Turning to Hank, Cal adjusted his tan Stetson by the brim. "If you see any new breaks in the fence or something doesn't look right, you give me a call."

Two days later Hank found an opening in a cross-fence between the Drexlers' land and Tutan's. No breaks. No cuts. This time, the fence had been taken down from the posts. It could easily be put back up, and no one would be the wiser. Was that the plan?

He swung down from Ribsy's saddle for a closer look when a distant rifle shot nearly caused him a long walk back to the house.

"Easy, girl."

He'd nearly calmed her down before another shot was fired and he opted for an awkward running remount over losing the reins. He loped the mustang in a tight circle to distract her from taking off across the flat, which was what her one-track mind was set on. He started to head back the way he had come— no way would the mare go along with any human-brained investigation—when he noticed a small carcass. Prairie dog. *Dogs.* He counted five. He'd ridden into their little town and found carnage.

Another distant gunshot.

"Easy, Ribs."

Who in hell would be shooting prairie dogs in a wildlife sanctuary?

Damn Tootin'. Who the hell else? Hank wondered how many hands he hired to keep his ranch going while he ran around playing games.

He had a pretty good idea where the shots were coming from. He'd taken a ride out this way, noticed a couple of dog towns and thought he'd come back sometime with a pair of binoculars and watch the big birds make meat. He could watch hawks and eagles all day long. But little men with big shotguns? Not so much.

Hank headed for high ground, following the fence line. The scrub brush on the bluffs hid him from the rider of an ATV pushing through the draw below with a discordant whine that set Hank's teeth on edge. Then he saw the rider's game. He was running horses. He was terrorizing a band of four mares, three foals and a stud. And the stud was Don Quixote. A shot rang out, and the horses flew past. Hank looked down and saw the rifle barrel and a green baseball cap at least a hundred yards below.

With a little backtracking he was able to circle behind the shooter without being seen or heard.

Leaving Ribsy ground-tied a few yards behind enemy lines, Hank was able to get close enough to count coup or cause a coronary. With luck, both.

"Going hunting, Mr. Tutan?"

Hank gave himself a moment to enjoy the look of a man who'd just heard a ghost. His brother favored their father in looks and build, but Hank had the voice. Not that John Night Horse had been much of a talker, but whenever he showed up in church, he always sang his heart out. Tutan's eyes bulged in a ruddy face gone pasty as he looked right and left, searching for the voice's owner.

"What's in season this time of year?" Hank stepped out from behind a scraggly clutch of chokecherry bushes.

"It's you." Tutan clapped his hand over his eyes. The color drained from his lips, and Hank had to wonder whose luck was in play. If the man keeled over, Hank might have to find a new profession. "Damn, you scared me," Tutan gasped.

"Did you take me for someone else, Mr. Tutan?" He said the name the way he'd heard it long ago, with his father's distinctive inflection.

"Night Horse," Tutan said carefully. "What was he to you?"

"I'll tell you what he wasn't." Hank raised his chin. "He wasn't a hunter. Had no patience for it. Didn't own a gun. Said he'd eaten enough deer meat growing up to last him a lifetime."

Tutan's eyes narrowed. "You don't look much like him."

"What happened to him?"

"Sounds like you know more about him than I do."

"Maybe." Hank nodded toward the draw. "That's quite a horse, isn't it?"

"Which one?"

"The one you're gunnin' for."

"They're protected. They're good for nothin' but making trouble, but the law says you gotta leave 'em alone. Even when they run right through your fence." Tutan hefted his rifle as though he'd just remembered he had it with him. He wore a loaded hunter's vest over his white T-shirt. "What's not protected is those damn prairie dogs. It's open season on those sonsabitches."

"You're running those horses."

"I don't know who that is on the four-wheeler. Figured it must be one of Sally's people. Or Annie's. Or yours, maybe." He turned his head and spat. "I'm shooting prairie dogs."

"You're on the wrong side of the fence."

"They're the ones on the wrong side of the fence." He shouldered his rifle and pointed it toward the foot of the hill. "Look down there. See? I hit one, two, three. Oops. Still twitching." He aimed and fired. "That's four. They're pests. They destroy good pasture. A cow, a horse, she steps in one of those holes and *snap* goes the leg. She's all done." He turned and squinted up at Hank. "Fence is down again. Bet you've got horses scattered from here to Texas." He nodded toward the low ground. "Those prairie dogs don't give a rat's ass whose side of the fence they dig up. Horses don't care about fences. Why should I?"

"Because you're claiming to be the injured party."

"*That's* an injured party." Tutan waved his rifle at the dead prairie dogs and laughed. "Tell the Drexler girls they don't have to thank me. It's something I like to do in my spare time."

"Anything happens to that horse, I'm comin' after you."

Tutan tucked the butt of his rifle into his armpit, pointing the barrel at the ground. He gave a cold smile. "I'll leave the light on for you."

Nothing riled Hank more than a mean-spirited smile.

Sally stared at her stick. She hadn't used it in two and a half months—*months*—but she could've used it today. After getting her fingers tied up in tack and caught once in a drawer, once in a cupboard door, she'd pronounced herself "all thumbs" and turned the job of straightening out the tack room over to a volunteer. She'd tripped over her own feet on the way back to the house, and she'd cursed the words and the placement of a rail fence four feet out of reach.

All thumbs. Numb thumbs would have been more accurate. But who would get it besides somebody like her? *Tripped over her own feet.* Normal people did that all the time. But normal people had no trouble getting back up.

A few more days. Was that too much to ask? Couldn't she be an ordinary, active, fully functional woman for just a few more days? A few more days living in a whole woman's body with the whole, healthy man whose boots were bringing him to her right now, across the wood floor in the foyer, into the hallway. She knew the measure of his stride, the sound of his boot heels, the feel of his presence in the house.

She hadn't wasted any time using her senses while the disease was sleeping. Maybe they'd given her more of him than she would want to be left with in his absence, but she wasn't about to back down. She turned, saw him standing there in her doorway, and willed herself—for the hundredth time since she'd last picked herself up when no one was looking, which meant it didn't count—to hold out just *a few more days.*

"Guess what." Springing from her desk chair like an eager school girl was a private test. Publicly passing, she smiled accordingly. "I just had a call from a guy named Logan Wolf Track. He's on the Tribal Council, and he's related to Kay Night Horse." She put her arms around him and gave a full-press squeeze, another personal best. "She already put in a good word for us."

"'Course she did. What did he say?"

"They'll be voting at their next meeting. He says

he's looked at our application, and he's quite familiar with the sanctuary. He's been up on the back roads, and he says he really likes the stallion, and that's a nice band of mares he's got running with him and all like that. So, I know he's on the horses' side, which is good. And I don't think he likes Tutan."

"Why not?"

"He didn't say it in so many words. It was kind of an oh-yeah-*that*-guy response. Maybe it was just a tone, but I got the distinct impression he's on our side." She laid her fingertip on his square chin. "So, thank you."

"Thank my sister-in-law."

"I did. I will again. And I won't pop any corks until after the vote is taken, but I'm feeling good about it."

"Yeah. That's…" Hands on her shoulders, he drew himself from her arms. She dropped them quickly to her sides and started her own withdrawal, but he caught her hand before it was complete. "The honeymooners should be back soon, huh?"

"In another week. But that doesn't mean…" She squeezed his hand despite her inclination to pull away. "You're free to go anytime you need to. Or want to."

"We still have to separate out those horses Kevin ran in off the road. We'll take care of that this morning." He rubbed his thumb over the back of her hand. He was trying to tell her something, but he was *all thumbs*. "But Kevin got them in without any help."

"Kevin's come a long way."

He met her gaze. "I just had a run-in with Tutan."

"The fence was down?"

"Yeah, but that's not the half of it. He was shooting prairie dogs."

"No law against that."

"On your property."

"Double D property?"

"Your side of the fence, where all those dog towns are."

"They've gotten out of control in that area on both sides of the fence. I haven't decided what to do about it."

"Is letting Tutan have at 'em one of the options?"

"Well, no, but I don't want you to—"

"Because whatever he's up to, it's about horses, not prairie dogs. Some young guy was runnin' your Spanish stud and his band up and down that draw, and Tutan's all gun happy. Then I come along, and he starts shootin' off his mouth."

"Oh, Hank. You two are fuse meets powder keg."

"No, we're not. He's nothing. No fire, no fire-power, *nothing*. But I'm not goin' anywhere until Zach gets back."

"Are you supposed to be somewhere else?"

"Doesn't matter."

"Are you scheduled for a rodeo this weekend?"

"I'm not goin' anywhere, and I'm not callin' anybody. I don't want you to, either. Let them take all the time they want. I'm just checking."

"They haven't changed their plans," she said quietly. "One more week. We'll call the sheriff, Hank. We'll be fine. You do what you need to do."

"I need to stay. I made Zach a promise. Hell, I made Tutan a promise. I need to be here until Zach comes back."

The weekend passed without incident. Not that there weren't happenings. Feel-good happenings—the kind Sally craved above all else—and concerning happenings, which she covered pretty well, she thought, keeping her concerns to herself. She would not bring the cane out until Hank left. He knew about it, but not firsthand. If she played her cards just right, she could preserve her dignity.

The feel-goods—or the good feels—were happening with delightful regularity. She pitted Little Henry against big Ribsy in a cutting contest, separating wild horses from a herd of watchful bovine mothers. Little Henry lost only because Sally lost her stirrups—actually lost her feet for a little while there, but the two of them were the only ones who knew. Under the circumstances, not losing her seat was a major, if private, victory. Cutting was a tricky feat for any rider, with her horse changing direction at the drop of a hat, stopping on a dime. Both mustangs had improved their cutting skills under Zach's hand in testament to Sally's claim that mustangs could be trained for almost anything.

Her aching butt was a glorious feeling. She hadn't put a horse through any real paces in a long time. Better to have ached and lost than never to have ached at all. But it was the moaning and groaning every time she sat down that brought her the best reward. Hank took her to his room, stripped her down, buttered her up with lotion, kneaded her muscles into putty, and made slow, sumptuous love to her until every nerve in her body grabbed a part in her physical version of the *Hallelujah Chorus*.

"I'm going to miss this," she told him as she lay in his arms, languidly stroking his hard, lean hip.

"That's not the part you'll miss. Come on."

"It's not the only part, but it's *part* of the part. They're bolted together." She stroked him, back to front. "Without the bolt, you'd lose your screw."

"Naughty girl." He grabbed hold of her bottom and pressed her against him. "Without the bolt, *you'd* lose *your* screw."

"And I would definitely miss that." She looked up at him in the dark. "I'm going to miss all of you. Especially your hands." She kissed his shoulder. "I love the way they feel on me. Anywhere, anytime. Your hands touching me makes me feel special."

"You are."

"A cool connection. A warm kinship."

He kissed her hair, the bump on her forehead, her nearly blind eye. Her heart fell. He had her deficiencies all mapped out. Except the hair. She had good hair. Knowing Hank, the hair kiss was a diversionary tactic. He knew her legs were about to start giving her real trouble again. Not so special. Very undignified.

"I hope we hear from the BLM about the training contest this week."

"I hope you do, too. I hope it works out."

"Thank you." That wasn't what she wanted to hear. "You don't have to…You know, you could just enter the contest. If you had the time." He tossed off a chuckle. "But I know you have places to go and people to see."

"I don't have a place to be, or people to see. What I have is a job. I have things to do. That's something you never run out of—never runs out on you. There's always something to do."

"Of course. I know exactly what you mean."

"If you need any help with your mustangs… You probably don't need much shoeing, but maybe with the contest…"

"If they approve."

"If they approve."

"Max Becker probably thinks I have a screw loose, just proposing such a thing."

"Your screws are none of Max Becker's goddamn

business." He braced up on one elbow and cupped her face in his other hand. "Not as long as I'm here."

Hoolie and Sally met the newlyweds at the Rapid City Airport. They came off the plane holding hands, still looking like they weren't about to come down from the clouds anytime soon.

"Getting from Sydney to New York was the easy part," Zach said. He looked tired, but at least part of the bleariness was clearly deliriousness. It was contagious. Sally felt a little dizzy herself.

"New York to South Dakota is the real stretch," Zach was saying. "But I could get used to that first-class treatment. They just keep pourin' on the bubbly."

"*That* explains it." Sally laughed. "And I thought you were still—"

"Except the Denver to Rapid City leg. That twenty-passenger egg crate, that's your reality check."

"The reality is, you're still married."

"Oh, yeah. It's official." Zach threw an arm around Hoolie's shoulders as they headed for baggage. "How's ol' Hank been makin' out?"

Hoolie nearly choked on his cherry Slurpee.

"You'll have to ask him," Sally said. "After I look up the directions for turning myself into a fly on the wall."

Zach gave his wife the high brow. "I'm thinkin' things went well."

"I'm thinking you don't know my sister."

On the way home, the women sat in the backseat of Zach's beloved pickup, Zelda Blue, and the men sat in the front, South Dakota style. Zach fondled Zelda's steering wheel, and Annie teased him about his separation anxiety every time they'd ridden in a foreign vehicle. Hoolie wanted to know if they'd seen any Australian "Brombies" like the horses in *The Man From Snowy River,* and Zach turned up the country music and sang along with Willie and Waylon and the boys.

Annie took pointed notice of her sister's cane. "How are you feeling?" she asked quietly.

It was the wrong question. Sally was neither ready nor willing to make up an answer.

Hank hated goodbyes. If he had anything to say about it, it wouldn't be the forever kind—he was planning on seeing Sally again, one way or another—but he didn't want to say goodbye to the time they'd shared. Even with the same woman, a guy never knew who he might be saying hello to the next time around.

He decided to be gone when the family got back. Let them tell their stories back and forth, show pictures, give out souvenirs. He'd give Sally a call tonight and explain. He just didn't want his last three weeks getting thrown into the mix with somebody else's honeymoon.

Before he headed for the Denver Stock Show, he

had one stop to make. He wanted to make an indelible impression on Tutan, make sure the man knew exactly who he was dealing with and that it wasn't time for counting because the dealing wasn't done.

Tutan was just toolin' into his yard on a familiar-looking ATV. Hank purposely parked in the man's road to let him know he was there for a powwow and got out of the pickup. A man with decent manners would have done the same, met in the middle and given his visitor a courteous ear. Not Damn Tootin'.

"Zach and Annie are coming home today," Hank shouted over the infernal small-engine racket.

"So?"

He nodded toward the yard light. "I saw your light on."

"It's always on," Tutan bellowed. "What's on your mind?"

"Shut this thing off and I'll tell you!"

Tutan complied, folded his arms across his barrel chest, and kept his seat.

"You got the news about the tribal leases?"

"I did. You can be damn sure it's not the final word. I've had those leases since—"

"It's the final word, Mr. Tutan. Indians love horses. There's no gettin' around that fact."

"So, you went to the tribe and said something about John Night Horse. Am I right? But he wasn't from this reservation, and neither are you. You got no right coming down here and making trouble over something that happened years ago."

Hank's blood ran cold, which kept him cool while he stared steely eyed through a red haze and spoke carefully measured words. "What *exactly* happened?"

"Nobody knows." Tutan gave an insolent shrug. "He'd been dead for who knows how long by the time they found him. Been drinking. Looked like he might've been hunting. Might've fallen on his gun. Might've…" He stared straight at Hank's face. "Who the hell knows?"

"And no one was with him."

"Might've been. Nobody ever came forward, so there's no way to find out, is there? It happened a long time ago." Tutan's eyes narrowed. "What was he to you?"

"He was my father."

"I figured as much. You should've told me right away. I know it's a little late, but you have my condolences."

Unable to look at the man any longer, Hank stared across Tutan's alfalfa field at the hills bolstering the blue horizon. He had what he wanted for now. Back to nature for Lakota land, open spaces for a few more wild horses.

"You still hold some Indian lease land," Hank reminded Tutan.

"That's right. And the way I heard it, I still have some support on the Council."

"You could lose the rest of your leases," Hank warned. "I'm not from this reservation, but we're all related. You mess with those mustangs, you'll regret it."

"I don't have time for horses."

"I do," Hank said quietly. "Not only that, I have time to make your life a living hell in ways you haven't thought of yet. You cause Sally Drexler trouble, I'll cause you trouble. I'll match you, and then I'll go you one worse. You've got friends? I've got friends. Plus I've got cause." He took a step back. "I don't know who killed my father, but you do. One way or another you'll take his death with you to your grave. *Sooner.* Or later. That's your problem."

"The hell you say." Tutan laughed. "I'm not superstitious."

"Neither am I." Hank's smile was cool and calculated. "You keep trying to kill Sally's sanctuary, you'll pay in *this* life, *Mr.* Tutan. And you'll pay dearly."

Hank watched the man and his little scooter shrink in his rearview mirror as he drove away. Regrets all around, he thought. He was already regretting his decision to leave.

But, hell, he had a job to do.

He jammed a CD into the slot in his dashboard and sang along with another Hank.

He was so lonesome he could cry.

Chapter Ten

Within a few months the new lease on tribal land would become the bridge between the Double D and the more isolated public land Sally hoped to add to the sanctuary. Tutan's leases were paid through October. After that, he was *outta there.*

Sally had it all now. Everything she and Hank had talked about—a place to be, people to see, a ton of work to do. Most of the work she had to do could be done on her place, and that was a good thing. She wasn't quite as limber as she had been when she'd last seen Hank about a month ago. *Exactly* a month ago if the month were February, which was what it felt like. Cold, barren, desolate—a feeling Sally kept bottled up while she served as a smiling Maypole for the newly-weds to chase around she couldn't have dampened Annie's and Zach's spirits even if she'd wanted to. And before Hank, she might have wanted to.

Before Hank, she might have retreated to her room and let them have the rest of the house, knowing full well that they would wonder and worry, at least a little. She always said she didn't want that. Now she meant it. She wanted what she had—a place to be, work to do and people to see. One in particular.

She glanced over Little Henry's rump and past the corral fence. The road was long and empty, but the place—*her* place—was shaping up the way she'd long dreamed. She was working on it. The round pen and the new bigger, better outdoor arena were already half finished. She worked on her people—volunteers were coming out of the woodwork since the training competition had been advertised.

She worked when she relaxed, if currying her new favorite mustang could be considered work. Little Henry loved attention, and she loved the way he smelled, the way he snuffled, the way his ears twitched, but mainly the way his hide felt against her palms. She liked the feel of feel. It made her feel alive.

She couldn't stand for hours on end anymore, and she'd stopped pushing it. Pretty much. Her cane stood ready to get her back to the house if a bout of no-feel threatened. Heat brought it on sometimes, but she loved the feel of the sun on her face. Stress could do it to her, but she hadn't heard from Damn Tootin' in more than a week.

Loneliness was a killer. Not literally, of course. She wasn't about to die from MS, and she could live without Hank Night Horse. He'd kept his promise, and he'd given her the best three weeks she'd had in years. She didn't blame him for taking off before she and Hoolie pulled in with the bride and groom. Who needed to ooh and aah over a thousand pictures of kangaroos and Australian ranches and horseback riding in the Outback? Hank, too, had places to be and people to see. Not to mention work to do. *Two* jobs. He was a busy man.

He'd called that night, said he'd just pulled into Denver.

"Hope I didn't wake you up," he said quietly. "I figured you'd all be up gabbing, but you sound…distant."

"I am distant. How far is it from here to Denver? I haven't been there in years."

"The Stock Show starts in a couple of days."

"A couple of days?"

"A guy called me—another PA—asked me to fill in for him. I owe him one."

"When did he call?" When he didn't answer, she felt foolish. She laughed a little. "I mean…I didn't know you'd be leaving so soon."

"It felt like the right time. You're back to a full house now."

"I wouldn't say that. It's a big house." *Say no more, Sally. You might look pathetic sometimes, but you never have to sound pathetic.* Jack up that voice. "But, hey, your work here is done."

"Yeah. Back to earning a paycheck."

"We didn't keep you from—"

"No. You didn't. I was…glad to help out."

She knew he was. Hank was an honest man. She loved that about him. Among other things. "If you ever feel like donating more time to a worthy cause…"

"You mean the horses?"

"All charity work here is tax deductible." She put on a happy face and gave a good ol' Sally laugh.

"Yeah." This was straight-shooter Hank she was talking to. No laughing matter. "I want to see you again."

"You know where to find me. The days of going down the road are pretty much over for me."

"You're in a good place, Sally. Doing good work."

"I know. I truly appreciate everything you did, Hank." She drew a deep breath. "Stop by whenever you can."

And that was that. She'd said she'd see him whenever. *See you when I see you.* And she meant it. She'd missed a lot of things in recent years. The rodeo was one of those things. Dancing, driving, getting from here to there without embarrassing herself were a few more things. Seeing clearly out of her right eye would have been nice. A man? Sure. Why not. Add Hank Night Horse to the list. When he came back through her corner of the world, maybe they could pick up where they left off for a day or two. If she felt like it.

If he came back.

Please come back.

She felt tired when she put the grooming bucket back in the tack room. She was glad she had her cane handy. She felt a few months of wheelchair rides coming on, but not, she hoped, before fall. Her right foot wanted to turn on her as she limped back to the corral with a feed pan full of oats for Little Henry. She should have used a bucket with a handle. It wouldn't be the first time she'd ended up face down in a pan of oats.

Nor the last. She called to the horse and laughed aloud when he came trotting toward her. She'd heard recently that several good belly laughs a day could make a huge improvement in a person's overall health, and her good ol' Sally laugh was always at the ready. She was all about improvement.

"Are you feeding my namesake?"

He startled her, but she kept her cool. No tripping over her own feet, no face in the oats. She turned, and her heart rate redoubled when she saw his handsome face.

"Can I help?" Hank asked.

"Thanks. I've got it." She hoped her smile wasn't

coming off all shaky. "You're sneaky, Hank Night Horse."

"I've got a reputation to protect."

"I'll spread the word."

He glanced at the horse inside the corral. "Doesn't look like he's been ridden."

"I've gotten lazy."

"Can't have that." He took the pan from her hand. "Little Henry should have to earn this."

"I'm really not up to—" She was nearly up to Hank's shoulders, swept off her feet by two strong arms. Like *that* would ever happen. "What are you doing, you crazy man?"

"We're going for a ride." He carried her to the fence. "Get the gate, will ya? I've got my arms full."

"I can't." But she did. She opened the gate. "I mean I shouldn't. Not—" He lifted her onto the horse's back like a sack of feed. "I'm gonna ride with a halter and lead rope?"

"Can you throw your leg over before you slide off and I have to lift you back up there?"

"You see, that's part of the prob—" He lifted her leg by the boot heel and gave her a leg over. She grabbed a handful of mane and scooted toward the withers while he made a rein from the lead. "Okay. But what's this *we* stuff?"

"Which is your good eye? Oh, yeah, the left. Watch over your left shoulder. You don't wanna miss this."

He took a step back and vaulted over Little Hank's rump almost faultlessly. There was one small *oomph*.

"Impressive performance," she allowed as he rested his chin on her left shoulder. "Of course, we named him *Little* Henry for a reason."

"And big Henry only does that trick once in a blue moon for a reason." He kissed her left cheek and whispered in her left ear. "There will be no second performance of any kind tonight."

She laughed. Hell, she was a woman. What did she know? Besides the fact that he had to be kidding.

"Just for that, I'm withholding the reach-around I was about to give you, too." But he did reach for the rein, and he pushed the open gate and nudged Little Henry with his boot heel. "I might as well tell you right up front—"

"I think you're riding what the drovers call drag."

"—that I'm crazy about you."

That shut her up. Briefly. "How do you know this?"

"I've been crazy before. Wasn't planning on goin' there again, but there it is." He slipped his free arm around her, sneaked his hand under the bottom of her T-shirt and spread his fingers over her bare skin. "Here's what I know. I truly appreciated everything *we* did. I appreciated falling asleep with you at night and sitting down to the table with you in the morning."

"Oh, come on. What about the part *before* the falling asleep?"

"That goes without saying." He chuckled. "I will say I appreciate your appreciation on that score."

"I did, didn't I?" She shivered as his little finger invaded her waistband. "You weren't easy, but I managed to score."

"I'm not easy with being crazy about somebody. Scares the hell out of me."

"So…how does this work, exactly?"

"Crazy doesn't really work. It just is." He tightened his arms around her as he guided Little Henry around the House that Zach built. "But if I work, and if you work, with any luck we can make crazy work. I can't just stop by. I want to be with you, Sally. All or nothing." She heard him swallow. Hard. "Of course, the feeling has to be mutual," he added softly.

"Oh, Hank." She let her head fall back and rest on his shoulder. "I have a disease—"

"I know."

"—that isn't going away."

"You're telling this to a halfways doctor?"

"You couldn't even tell."

"That's the half I'm missing."

"Sometimes…sometimes I look like a drunk staggering around because…"

"This is supposed to bother me?"

"Because I can't control what I can't feel, Hank!"

"What can't you feel, Sally?"

"My feet, my legs, my fingers sometimes. I told you, it's as unpredictable as…"

"You're unpredictable, with or without MS. And I'm as predictable as sunrise. I'm tellin' ya, it can work." He turned his lips to her temple. "I can't control what I *can* feel. And what I feel for you isn't going away. *Ever.*"

She closed her eyes. Her left one—the *good* one—leaked a damn tear.

And a pair of full, sweet lips kissed it away.

"Can you feel this?" he asked. And she turned her mouth to take the kiss she felt coming.

"You know what, Sally?"

"What?"

"Neither one of us is watching where we're going." She opened her eyes and drank the smile from his as he whispered, "This little mustang is one hell of a horse."

* * * * *

Rancher Ramsey Westmoreland's temporary cook is way too attractive for his liking. Little does he know Chloe Burton came to his ranch with another agenda entirely....

That man across the street had to be, without a doubt, the most handsome man she'd ever seen.

Chloe Burton's pulse beat rhythmically as he stopped to talk to another man in front of a feed store. He was tall, dark and every inch of sexy—from his Stetson to the well-worn leather boots on his feet. And from the way his jeans and Western shirt fit his broad muscular shoulders, it was quite obvious he had everything it took to separate the men from the boys. The combination was enough to corrupt any woman's mind and had her weakening even from a distance. Her body felt flushed. It was hot. Unsettled.

Over the past year the only male who had gotten her time and attention had been the e-mail. That was simply pathetic, especially since now she was practically drooling simply at the sight of a man. Even his stance—both hands in his jeans pockets, legs braced apart—was a pose she would carry to her dreams.

And he was smiling, evidently enjoying the conversation being exchanged. He had dimples, incredibly sexy dimples in not one but both cheeks.

"What are you staring at, Clo?"

Chloe nearly jumped. She'd forgotten she had a lunch date. She glanced over the table at her best friend from college, Lucia Conyers.

"Take a look at that man across the street in the blue shirt, Lucia. Will he not be perfect for Denver's first issue of *Simply Irresistible* or what?" Chloe asked with so much excitement she almost couldn't stand it.

She was the owner of *Simply Irresistible*, a magazine for today's up-and-coming woman. Their once-a-year Irresistible Man cover, which highlighted a man the magazine felt deserved the honor, had increased sales enough for Chloe to open a Denver office.

When Lucia didn't say anything but kept staring, Chloe's smile widened. "Well?"

Lucia glanced across the booth at her. "Since you asked, I'll tell you what I see. One of the Westmorelands—Ramsey Westmoreland. And yes, he'd be perfect for the cover, but he won't do it."

Chloe raised a brow. "He'd get paid for his services, of course."

Lucia laughed and shook her head. "Getting paid won't be the issue, Clo—Ramsey is one of the wealthiest sheep ranchers in this part of Colorado. But everyone knows what a private person he is. Trust me—he won't do it."

Chloe couldn't help but smile. The man was the epitome of what she was looking for in a magazine cover and she was determined that whatever it took, he would be it.

"Umm, I don't like that look on your face, Chloe. I've seen it before and know exactly what it means."

She watched as Ramsey Westmoreland entered the store with a swagger that made her almost breathless. She *would* be seeing him again.

Look for Silhouette Desire's
HOT WESTMORELAND NIGHTS
by Brenda Jackson,
available March 9 wherever books are sold.

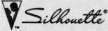

THE WESTMORELANDS

NEW YORK TIMES
bestselling author

BRENDA JACKSON

HOT WESTMORELAND NIGHTS

Ramsey Westmoreland knew better than to lust after the hired help. But Chloe, the new cook, was just so delectable. Though their affair was growing steamier, Chloe's motives became suspicious. And when he learned Chloe was carrying his child this Westmoreland Rancher had to choose between pride or duty.

Available March 2010 wherever books are sold.

Always Powerful, Passionate and Provocative.

SPECIAL EDITION

FROM *USA TODAY* BESTSELLING AUTHOR
CHRISTINE RIMMER

A BRIDE FOR JERICHO BRAVO

Marnie Jones had long ago buried her wild-child impulses and opted to be "safe," romantically speaking. But one look at born rebel Jericho Bravo and she began to wonder if her thrill-seeking side was about to be revived. Because if ever there was a man worth taking a chance on, there he was, right within her grasp....

Available in March
wherever books are sold.

Visit Silhouette Books at www.eHarlequin.com

SSE65511

HARLEQUIN *Presents*

Two families torn apart by secrets and desire
are about to be reunited in

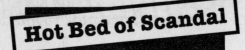

Hot Bed of Scandal

a sexy new duet by

Kelly Hunter

EXPOSED: MISBEHAVING WITH THE MAGNATE
#2905 Available March 2010

Gabriella Alexander returns to the French vineyard she
was banished from after being caught in flagrante with the
owner's son Lucien Duvalier—only to finish what they started!

REVEALED: A PRINCE AND A PREGNANCY
#2913 Available April 2010

Simone Duvalier wants Rafael Alexander and always has, but
they both get more than they bargained for when a night of
passion and a royal revelation rock their world!

HP12905

HARLEQUIN
Ambassadors

Want to share your passion for reading Harlequin® Books?

Become a Harlequin Ambassador!

Harlequin Ambassadors are a group of passionate and well-connected readers who are willing to share their joy of reading Harlequin® books with family and friends.

You'll be sent all the tools you need to spark great conversation, including free books!

All we ask is that you share the romance with your friends and family!

You'll also be invited to have a say in new book ideas and exchange opinions with women just like you!

To see if you qualify* to be a Harlequin Ambassador, please visit **www.HarlequinAmbassadors.com.**

*Please note that not everyone who applies to be a Harlequin Ambassador will qualify. For more information please visit www.HarlequinAmbassadors.com.

Thank you for your participation.

BAP09BPA

REQUEST YOUR FREE BOOKS!

2 FREE NOVELS PLUS 2 FREE GIFTS!

SPECIAL EDITION

Life, Love and Family!

YES! Please send me 2 FREE Silhouette® Special Edition® novels and my 2 FREE gifts (gifts are worth about $10). After receiving them, if I don't wish to receive any more books, I can return the shipping statement marked "cancel." If I don't cancel, I will receive 6 brand-new novels every month and be billed just $4.24 per book in the U.S. or $4.99 per book in Canada. That's a saving of 15% off the cover price! It's quite a bargain! Shipping and handling is just 50¢ per book in the U.S. and 75¢ per book in Canada.* I understand that accepting the 2 free books and gifts places me under no obligation to buy anything. I can always return a shipment and cancel at any time. Even if I never buy another book from Silhouette, the two free books and gifts are mine to keep forever.

235 SDN E4NC 335 SDN E4NN

Name	(PLEASE PRINT)	
Address		Apt. #
City	State/Prov.	Zip/Postal Code

Signature (if under 18, a parent or guardian must sign)

Mail to the Silhouette Reader Service:
IN U.S.A.: P.O. Box 1867, Buffalo, NY 14240-1867
IN CANADA: P.O. Box 609, Fort Erie, Ontario L2A 5X3

Not valid for current subscribers to Silhouette Special Edition books.

Want to try two free books from another line?
Call 1-800-873-8635 or visit www.morefreebooks.com.

* Terms and prices subject to change without notice. Prices do not include applicable taxes. N.Y. residents add applicable sales tax. Canadian residents will be charged applicable provincial taxes and GST. Offer not valid in Quebec. This offer is limited to one order per household. All orders subject to approval. Credit or debit balances in a customer's account(s) may be offset by any other outstanding balance owed by or to the customer. Please allow 4 to 6 weeks for delivery. Offer available while quantities last.

Your Privacy: Silhouette is committed to protecting your privacy. Our Privacy Policy is available online at www.eHarlequin.com or upon request from the Reader Service. From time to time we make our lists of customers available to reputable third parties who may have a product or service of interest to you. If you would prefer we not share your name and address, please check here. ☐

Help us get it right—We strive for accurate, respectful and relevant communications. To clarify or modify your communication preferences, visit us at www.ReaderService.com/consumerschoice.

SSE10